PRAISE FOI
NICHOL~~~ ~~~~~~

Death Never Sleeps
Michael Nicholas, Book 1

"The story takes nerve-wracking turns . . . A fine technological thriller that only gets better as it goes along."
- Kirkus Reviews

"A story of murder, betrayal and love with twists and turns that as a professional detective even I didn't expect . . . A Must Read! E.J. Simon is the real deal."
- Vito Colucci, Jr., author of *Rogue Town*

"Some stories take a bit to get going, this one pulls you right in and keeps you engaged. Interesting characters, quick paced story and unpredictable plot are the main highlights. Can't wait to read the next one!"
- CBS, Amazon

"I loved the premise of the book and the way the author develops the story. Set at the start of the AI concept introduction to the world, EJ Simon structured his story with believable characters, strong character development, and a credible story line. ... This is a fast-paced thriller that's hard to put down."
- Richard J. Oberhofer, Amazon

"Simon takes a crime story—and then creates an even more thrilling drama around one of the main characters who duplicated himself on his computer—just before he was murdered. The author lightens the story too by including many scenes in real restaurants and locations around the world. A very unique and well-written story."

- Luke Scott, Goodreads

"E. J. Simon masterfully crafts a narrative that keeps readers on the edge of their seats, blending complex characters, international settings, and technological intrigue. The dynamic between Michael and Alex, so different yet bound by blood, adds depth and emotion to the series. The writing is sharp and engrossing, with unexpected twists and turns that keep readers guessing until the very end."

- Vikash Khokhar, Amazon

Death Logs In
Michael Nicholas, Book 2

"The novel teems with subplots ... But Simon expertly manages these various storylines, and they help maintain an impressive pace .... An action-laden plot and another open ending will have the series collecting many more fans."
- Kirkus Reviews

"E.J. Simon brings the future of artificial intelligence to present day in *Death Logs In*. This is a new breed of crime thriller."
- Vito Colucci, Jr., author of *Rogue Town*

"This is a very well-crafted novel with good suspense, characters, and plot twists. The presentation of an artificial-intelligence character took an excellent imagination and clever writing. I thoroughly enjoyed this novel and highly recommend it."
- Ed Sheehan, Goodreads

"When you can't wait to sneak the next chapter's read between meetings, you know this book is a 'must read.'"
- Cherie, Amazon

"The mystery and suspense gets more intense as everything unfolds. I just could not keep from being intrigued. I had to know what would happen next. The twists and turns are not at all predictable. ... This is one of the most uniquely written thrillers I have ever read."
- Amy, Goodreads

Death Logs Out
Michael Nicholas, Book 3

"*Death Logs Out* is an incredibly suspenseful and captivating thriller that is built on tension, drama, and character developments that will have readers logging in for the rest of the series."

- The Reading Corner for All, Goodreads

"There is something about Simon's writings that make you think you are right there. [*Death Logs Out*] is not only entertaining, but gives you something to think about. I recommend all his books."

- PTF, Amazon

"This is a book which jumps right into action and simply doesn't stop, but occasionally it takes a breath and raises awareness of ethical topics involving artificial intelligence. While *Death Logs Out* can be read on its own, it would be a shame not to read *Death Never Sleeps* and *Death Logs In*, wherein Alex's character further embraces life in both human and artificial forms. It is a fun read by an author whose books just get better and better."

- H and H Franklin, Amazon

"Another winner by E.J. Simon. Timely, believable, gripping and leaves you wanting more."

- MMSIG, Amazon

"[*Death Logs Out*] … continues the fast-paced thrills with a plot that combines mystery, technology, and crime. It's a very entertaining ride with lots of twists and turns. While not directly discussing them, it does provoke interesting questions about the nature of identity. …Very entertaining and satisfying reads."

- Steve, Goodreads

"As in real life, most of the characters aren't just good or evil, they're complex and unpredictable. It was difficult to put this book down, and I probably would have read it in one sitting if my eyes had allowed it."

- Dawn H, Amazon

Death in the Cloud
Michael Nicholas, Book 4

"The book rockets along at a rapid clip, but E. J. Simon doesn't sacrifice his characters for action—they're all interesting if not very likable people, from Alex's put-upon brother, Michael, and his wife Samantha, to Alex's bimbo of an ex-wife. Simon manages the trick of getting you to care for them—well, all except for the neo-Nazis. This is not the first book in this series, but it stands on its own quite well, and I'll be looking for more by the author."

 - A. L. Sirois, Goodreads

"A true master of words who bring characters to life in your own world urging you to turn the page, order a fancy bottle of wine or travel the globe. Intrigue, twists, turns all in real time."

 - Margot Connor, Amazon

"I really enjoyed reading this action packed novel that had me on the edge of my seat throughout. The situations and characters are believable and exciting. The writing and plot are fast and furious. The mystery and suspense are compelling."

 - David Morgan, Goodreads

"This book is such a wild ride! . . . if you like thrillers, twists and turns, and enemies hidden around every corner then this is the book for you!"

 - It's Kawaii PC, Amazon

"This novel has a unique, fast paced, gripping plot line. The characters are chiseled with depth and detail and the story gripped me from the start. I was taken on a whirl wind of ups and downs, ins and outs as I followed the uniqueness of this political thriller. Think Artificial Intelligence meets White House Down with the intensity, the twists and turns and the jaw dropping moments. Definitely a book I will read again and again!"

- Molly J, Amazon

DEATH IN THE KREMLIN

MICHAEL NICHOLAS, BOOK 5

E. J. SIMON

Book cover design by ebooklaunch.com
Book interior design by Bookery

Published in the United States of America by Simon/Zef Publishing
Paperback ISBN: 978-1-7371480-0-5
E-book ISBN: 978-1-7371480-1-2

*Dedicated to Professors George Crutchfield
and Lloyd Brown, who, surely against
their better judgment, had faith in me.*

FOREWORD

I began writing *Death in the Kremlin* in 2018 and was almost ready to publish it when Putin's troops invaded Ukraine. I had never intended for my fictional version of him to be a hero, but the real-life Putin's real-life actions disrupted my writing in ways I never expected.

First, I became distracted. By his actions, the almost daily reports of his impending downfall, terminal illness, insanity, you name it.

Next I became consumed with a depressing and constant stream of new information on this character and what he was doing. There could simply be no way I would attempt to show a softer or even more human side to this man. As a result, I felt I had to change the arc of his character in my book, removing all possibility of redemption.

That's why the book's release has been delayed so many times.

But now it's done and you're about to read it. Thank you for being patient, and I hope you find it as satisfying to read as I did to write.

E.J. Simon
September 2024

"If a man die, shall he live again?
—Job 14: 14

"There is no more profound human bias than the expectation that tomorrow will be like today . . . Typically, that has been possible in human history. I don't think it is now."
—Ezra Klein, *This Changes Everything*
(on artificial intelligence)

CHAPTER 1

Michael Nicholas wanted to live a normal life. Four days after the murder of his brother, three years prior, he learned that "normal" would be impossible.

Sitting in his spacious glass-walled Manhattan corporate office, he scanned the page he'd ripped out of the New York *Daily Mirror* the day after his brother died:

Notorious NY Gambling Figure
Gunned Down in Queens Restaurant

Alex Nicholas, a notorious New York underworld figure, was murdered last night in a Queens restaurant as he dined with the proprietor. The lone gunman was shot and killed by off-duty police officers as he continued to fire his handgun at Mr. Nicholas. Both were pronounced dead at the scene.

Mr. Nicholas, sixty, was a popular figure in the neighborhood and often dined at Grimaldi's, a local restaurant and bar he once owned. Despite his reputation as the head of one of the largest illegal gambling and loan-sharking operations in the city, he was beloved by locals and respected by the many police officers who frequented the restaurant. "He was a tough guy with a big heart," one officer at the scene said. He was said to help people who had fallen on hard times or gone through crises, such as drug addiction.

According to a police spokesman, the murder appeared to have the earmarks of a professional "hit," although the motive remains unknown.

Nicholas is survived by his third wife, Donna, his son George, and his brother, Michael Nicholas, the chief executive officer of Gibraltar Financial, a *Fortune* 500 corporation based in New York City.

Michael tucked the article back into his briefcase, turned around in his sleek white leather Eames desk chair, and gazed out the floor-to-ceiling windows of his fortieth floor office. He watched the ribbon of rush hour traffic, a line of taillights stretching up Madison Avenue, as far as he could see. Soon it would be time to go.

Interrupting his thoughts, Karen DiNardo, his longtime executive assistant, appeared by his desk, holding out an envelope and a manila file folder with an inch-thick stack of neatly fastened pages inside.

"Here are your airline tickets—you're flying Delta. I printed them out, along with the latest research I put together for you on artificial intelligence. Your car to LaGuardia is waiting downstairs and your bags have already arrived at your beach house. Don't forget your license." She checked her watch. "Don't you think you need to get going?"

"Yes, I'll be on my way in five minutes. Are there any newsworthy developments in the file?"

"You'll have to decide for yourself when you read it. It looks like soon there won't be anything that artificial intelligence won't be able to do better than humans, except maybe sex. And now that I think of it, maybe not even that."

"That's good to know. Thanks for sharing." Michael laughed as he loosened his tie.

"Seriously though," she said, "the big question appears to be whether artificial intelligence will ever be able to create or duplicate *consciousness*, your inner life, your awareness, a person's *mind*. But I don't want to take all the fun out of your reading material."

Michael already knew the answer.

She eyed him suspiciously, which was not unusual. "I'm sure one day, when you're ready, you'll tell me what this fascination with AI is all about. I know it must have something to do with your late brother, since it was right after he passed that you got interested in this tech."

Michael nodded, ignoring the bait. "There's one more thing I need to do and then I'll be on my way."

"Okay, but don't push it; traffic to LaGuardia is never good this time of day. Your driver just pulled up downstairs." DiNardo retreated to her own office, closing the frosted thick glass door behind her.

He waited to be sure she didn't pop right back in as she so often did with a question she forgot to ask or a last remark she needed to make. Then he reached for his computer.

It wasn't only his brother's murder that troubled Michael. It was what would happen when he signed into his laptop.

CHAPTER 2

Michael opened his laptop and, as he'd done so many times over the past three years, clicked on the gold icon of the Byzantine Orthodox cross, then typed in the secret password.

Almost instantly, the image appeared, a face looking remarkably like his own but ten years older, staring back at him.

Michael . . .

It's not unusual for two brothers to be completely different human beings, but Michael and Alex Nicholas had been as different as life and death. Now they were the living and the dead, respectively. And literally.

Friends and colleagues told Michael he reminded them of *Mad Men*'s Don Draper—a compliment, he hoped. Meanwhile, Alex had drawn comparisons to famous gangsters—most recently Tony Soprano—for both his personality and, to a degree, his appearance.

Michael was buttoned down, dressing in dark blue corporate suits, custom Turnbull & Asser white shirts, and ties from Charvet in Paris. Alex's sport coats had also been custom made, but they were flashier, with brighter colors, created by his tailor, Sung-Ho in Flushing, in return for forgiveness of Sung-Ho's frequent gambling debts.

They both grew up in the same home with the same parents, nearly ten years apart, but while Michael had no clearly discernible accent, Alex sounded like Brooklyn, Italy, and the Mafia. In fact, he'd been none of that. His manner of speaking belied his private school education.

They both had engaging smiles. Michael's was inviting; Alex's could be wolfish, yet it still drew you in.

Michael possessed a CNN-ready grasp of current affairs and was known to prefer books to people since when he was a child. Alex shunned reading but could make lightning-fast mathematical calculations, an invaluable trait for a bookie. He could interpret numbers, odds, and point spreads and then tell you who owed him how much dough down to the penny, off the top of his head. Alex looked at books primarily while on the toilet.

Michael was a thinker, Alex a fighter. But despite the differences, they cherished each other, their shared upbringing, and their common history.

Although the words were never uttered during their nearly fifty years together, they loved each other.

"Hey, Alex," Michael greeted his dead brother.

CHAPTER 3

Alex Nicholas never believed in God. Until he died.

And even now he wasn't sure.

All those Sundays . . . forced to attend church. Worse, the services were mostly in Greek. All his young life, he mocked the hypocrisy of the grandiose priests with their towering hats and flowing, gold-speckled robes who claimed to have inside connections to the afterlife.

And then he was murdered. Yet there he remained. He'd never really believed that he could wake up from *that*.

But despite what his logical brain kept insisting, Alex was . . . awake . . . perhaps even alive.

At times he wondered whether it was a dream: the old Queens restaurant, his plate of veal parmigiana, speaking with Michael on his cell phone, the approaching gunman, the flash and earsplitting blast of the shots that just kept coming, his blood streaking across the plate, the other patrons staring at him while the body bag was zipped up over his head, the gurney, the dreaded medical examiner, the casket, the funeral, the cemetery he already knew too well, thorny roses tossed his way, dropping into the earth, the sound of the dirt hitting the roof of the casket. And then the silence while everyone else dispersed to their cars and set out for *his* wake, leaving him behind . . . alone . . . dead yet fully conscious and more alert than ever, in a muddy cemetery surrounded by others who were truly dead.

He kept waiting for that moment in the morning when he would open his eyes and see the familiar ceiling of his bedroom, dream over. But it never happened.

Instead, a hundred or more mourners filed into his favorite Long Island steakhouse, Bryant & Cooper. They set a place for him at the head table, ordered him a Dewar's, and a medium rare filet mignon with fries and lots of ketchup on the side. It would sit there, untouched, until his son George took it home—except for the Dewar's—and had it for lunch the next day.

They raised a toast to his empty place at the table, told stories about him, laughed, maybe even shed a hidden tear, talked about his gruff, tough personality and his soft heart, his craziness, his anger at anyone who crossed him and his unfailing generosity toward those in need or in trouble, a trait they'd never mentioned to his face when he was alive.

Secretly, he was sure, many mourners were relieved not to have to pay him the money they owed.

He still didn't understand how this state of cognizance, of consciousness, happened and how he had come to . . . exist once again. Or, for that matter, *where* it was that he now lived or if that was even the correct word to describe his state of awareness. But he knew he was conscious, and this was no dream. He was dead yet awake.

Seeing Michael again gave him the reassurance that he was alive.

CHAPTER 4

New York City

The notification that he had an incoming FaceTime call chimed on his computer. Checking the frosted glass to be sure no one was approaching his office door, Michael leaned in closer to his laptop and looked back at his brother.

"Someone found out about me and is trying to hack into my software."

"What do you think is going on? What are they looking to do?"

"Who the hell knows? Maybe they want to live forever in the cloud too. Maybe it's a terrorist or one of those crypto crazies."

"So you have no idea who's doing it?" Michael said, nervously glancing again at the door and then checking his watch.

"He—or she or it—is Russian, that's all I know. The attacks on my software are coming from a Russian site. I just don't know who's behind it."

"So, what does this mean? What do we do? What can I do?"

"For one thing, I wouldn't travel right now. I'd stay in the city. You'll be safer there."

Michael lowered the volume on his laptop. "I've got to go. Samantha's down there waiting for me and I have commitments. I can't cancel at the last minute; other people are counting on me. I have a legitimate day job if you recall, not just the one running your old business. And I can't exactly say that my dead brother warned me not to go."

"I'm not exactly dead."

"I understand that—I think—but no one else will. Anyway, what have the attacks on your software got to do with my traveling to North Carolina?"

"In order to duplicate someone, like what happened to me, they have to get the source codes behind my software. If they can't successfully hack into my codes, which they haven't been able to do so far, they have only two other options."

"Okay . . . what are the two options?"

"They could try and find those nerds—or the geniuses—I hired from Silicon Valley who put me in this state. That might be tough, though, since the last I heard they took the money I paid them and disappeared, which was part of our agreement. And they certainly don't need money now. Plus, they're scared to death, literally, about being discovered for any number of reasons besides their agreement with me. So getting to them will be tough, even for Russians."

"What's the second option?'

"The second option might be a lot easier."

"Yeah? What is it?"

"That they find *you*. If they capture your laptop, that would get them halfway there, but they still couldn't get the source codes. Not without my help. I'd have to unlock them."

"Seems like the codes are pretty secure. Right?"

Alex shook his head and smirked. He looked annoyed or impatient. "You know, for someone with all that fancy education and all the reading you do, sometimes you're not so smart."

"What do you mean?"

"Yeah, I'm not about to volunteer the source codes to someone who steals your laptop and let them delete me."

"Exactly—" Michael began.

"Unless . . . they happen to take—meaning *kidnap—you* along with your laptop, and then hold a knife to your throat until I agree to give up the codes."

Michael took a moment to let that sink in. As much as he missed his living brother and appreciated the fact that he still had a virtual one, he wished he could live a normal life, one without the constant need to keep his brother's presence a secret from everyone but his wife or the duplicity of running Alex's lucrative but illegal betting operation while also heading up a major and legitimate financial services corporation. Now it appeared that he was about to get embroiled in a potential life-and-death struggle with Russian hackers.

"Well," Michael said, "if that ever happened, you know, someone threatening to kill me unless you released the codes—"

"You'd be a dead man," Alex interrupted with a disturbingly straight face and then began to laugh. "Just kidding." He paused again, no longer smiling. "I think."

Michael was sure that the human brother he knew would never allow his younger brother's life to be at risk. But he silently wondered, would the *virtual* Alex, a creation of the secret breakthrough in artificial intelligence, act the same way?

Michael could see Karen's image, blurred through the frosted glass walls of his office. Surely coming to rush him along.

"I've got to go," Michael told his brother.

But before he signed out, Alex warned him one last time: "Don't get on that plane."

CHAPTER 5

Leaving through the revolving glass doors of the Gibraltar Financial offices on Madison Avenue, Michael spotted the black Cadillac limousine parked in the street with a "Nicholas" sign in the window.

As he approached the car he nodded to the driver and waved him away when he began to move to open the door for him. He placed his briefcase on the small table and settled into the backseat for the twenty-minute trip LaGuardia Airport. He made a mental note to remind Karen that he preferred a simpler and less ostentatious town car for his next ride. Nevertheless, he was pleased to see that his passenger compartment was sealed off from the driver's space.

He had arranged for his wife, Samantha, to pick him up at the Wilmington, North Carolina, airport, after which they would make the twenty-minute drive to their beach house at Kure Beach. Michael had his heart set on the veal parm at Freddie's tonight.

Feeling securely sealed in his bubble, he settled back into his seat and watched the city go by as the car headed up Madison Avenue toward FDR Drive in the direction of the RFK Bridge—formerly the Triborough Bridge—and Queens. But his view was interrupted by an incoming FaceTime call. It was Alex. He considered letting it go but, after a hesitation, accepted the video call, opening his laptop instead of taking it on his mobile.

Alex started speaking immediately. "Hey, I tracked down the hackers, the ones trying to get into my software."

"Really? So who are they?"

"They're Russian as I suspected, but I was able to pinpoint the exact location of their computers."

"What good's that going to do you?" Michael said, his eyes drifting to the driver's compartment for any sign that he might be able to overhear his conversation. "It's not exactly like you know your way around Russia."

"Let me narrow it down for you. The hacker or hackers are in Moscow."

"That really does narrow it down," Michael said sarcastically. "Moscow, we know it well."

"I have the exact location, actually two locations now."

"Great, you can FedEx them a cease-and-desist letter warning them that you know where they work and they'd better stop."

"The first address is 1/3 Bolshaya Lubyanka Street in Moscow."

"Interesting," Michael said, still somewhat disinterested. "Do you know who lives there or if it's an office?"

E.J. SIMON

"Yeah. It's the home of the FSB, Russia's successor to the KGB."

That got Michael's attention. "Seriously? . . . I'm afraid to ask where the second location is."

"Yeah, it gets better. 23, Ulitsa Ilyinka."

"That doesn't ring a bell—"

"It didn't to me either until I looked it up."

"Okay, what is it?" Michael asked anxiously.

"It's the Kremlin."

As though on cue, the locks of the rear doors clicked, unlocking and then locking again. Michael looked up to the driver's rearview mirror, catching a glimpse of the driver, who appeared to be watching him. Their eyes met.

And it was at that moment that Michael noticed a fine mist coming through the vents in the backseat compartment.

CHAPTER 6

Thirty thousand feet over the Baltic Sea

Michael Nicholas gazed out the window at the rapidly passing clouds in the muted moonlit evening sky. He was unsure of many things, but at this moment he wondered how long he had slept—or been unconscious—and how he happened to be alone in the plush cabin of a private jet instead of the Delta commuter flight from LaGuardia to Wilmington. Most of all, he wondered where it was taking him.

Turning his head, he stared at his open laptop computer on the burlwood table in front of him. The still image of his murdered brother stared back at him, a reminder of the other great uncertainty he faced. Alex's death had unveiled for Michael an awesome secret. One that had changed his life and world forever. He'd thought it a secret, but clearly, hostile parties had ferreted out the brothers' secret.

He looked around him, pressed his hands about his body until he felt the seat belt buckled at his waist. He was strapped into a soft, fine grained white leather seat, still dressed in the navy-blue suit and gray tie he'd worn to the office.

He tried to retrace his steps, his movements, the ones that had led him to where he now found himself. But he could only recall a vague collection of seemingly disparate film stills, scenes flickering back to him, not in any chronological order. Snippets and mini-flashbacks . . .

He remembered being in his office, meeting with his secretary, the file she handed him on . . . yes, the one on artificial intelligence . . . a limousine waiting for him on Madison Avenue. . . . Then his memory movie showed a blank screen. He kept trying to reverse the film, to play it back in slow motion, to find missing pieces to connect the dots, anything that might clue him in to exactly what had gotten him here.

His mind swung from the recent past to the sights and sounds around him: a soft whirring of jet engines, the muted sounds of speeding through the air, puffy clouds passing quickly outside the window, a single flashing red beacon like an ominous warning on the wing, two white leather seats facing his, another burlwood table separating them, rich dark-wood paneled walls, gray carpeting, and . . . a closed door to the cockpit.

He unbuckled his seat belt and rose from his chair, his legs and back aching from immobility. He glanced around the cabin: another empty single seat, four more identical ones around a conference table, a closed door with a small sign indicating an unoccupied lavatory, a small galley, eerily empty.

The only sign of life was a nearly empty bottle of vodka and a single shot glass with a small amount of a clear liquid sitting on the galley counter.

He walked through the cabin, holding on to the vacant seats along the way, until he reached the bulkhead, on which was displayed an electronic map of the world like the ones he'd seen on the entertainment screens on commercial airliners.

He moved in closer as the map disappeared and a series of slides took its place:

- Altitude: 34,800 feet
- Speed: 605 mph
- Outside temperature: -55 degrees C
- Time at departure position: 11:05 pm
- Time at destination: 7:05 am
- Arrival time: 7:26 am
- Time to destination: 21 minutes

Michael stared closely at the solid red line indicating the jet's path and the dot showing its current position in the sky.

He was currently over the Baltic Sea. And headed east.

He moved in closer, within inches of the screen, and tried to follow the dotted red line indicating the remainder of the trip. But before he could pinpoint the destination on the map, the screen changed again: "ETA: 0 hours, 19 min."

He would land in nineteen minutes. But where? He waited through the changing screens until the map reappeared.

This time he was prepared to trace the unfinished route to its destination. He followed it with the tip of his finger, carefully, moving his forefinger to the right, or east on the map, tracing the designated course until it ended, with a bold red star indicating the aircraft's destination.

Michael removed his finger from the screen, stepped back, took a deep breath, and looked again at the red star.

He was headed to Moscow.

He turned and made for the cockpit door.

CHAPTER 7

Michael approached the closed cockpit door.

Figuring it would be locked, he decided to knock first, but just as he lifted his arm, he changed his mind and instead placed his ear to the door.

There were no sounds coming from inside, although Michael felt a sudden vibration coursing through the frame of the aircraft and up to his shoes.

He slowly turned the handle on the door, and to his surprise, he could feel the door give. It was unlocked.

He opened it slightly . . . waited a few seconds and then opened it just enough to get a look inside the cockpit.

Only one of the two seats, the one on the left, was occupied. He could see the broad back of a dark-suited figure, a man, wearing a captain's hat with a gold braid.

The pilot turned around, unfazed and untroubled by Michael's presence. His eyes were focused elsewhere, somewhere beyond Michael.

Before a single word was exchanged, Michael felt a muscular forearm come around his neck from behind, squeezing his throat closed, and wrench him out of the cockpit and back into the passenger cabin.

CHAPTER 8

Dmitri Bogomolov, a young technology expert attached to the FSB, the Russian successor to the KGB, sat at his desk in the small nondescript office in FSB headquarters, his unruly dark hair giving him an unkempt aura, although no descriptor could have been further from the truth.

He wore a heavy cable-knit sweater to keep him warm. The thermostat in his office read a chilly seventeen degrees Celsius. Through the small rectangular window, he could view one of the snowcapped towers of the Kremlin, illuminated in the evening by massive floodlights, catching the steady blanket of wind-blown falling snow and reminding Bogolomov of the stage set for his favorite opera, *La Boheme*.

Tonight, Bogomolov's attention was focused on his desktop computer screen as he listened to the CNN international news broadcast:

"U.S. President Harry O'Brien today acknowledged that hackers, acting on behalf of a foreign government—almost certainly a Russian intelligence agency—broke into key government networks, including the Homeland Security, Treasury and Defense Departments, and gained free access to their email systems.

"It is a measure of the sudden panic sweeping U.S. government agencies that the Department of Homeland Security ordered all agencies to immediately shut down any use of a complex piece of network management software installed on the federal government's networks.

"But it was clearly too late, since the Russian hackers have had free rein for much of the year, according to experts, although it is not known how many networks they entered.

"The motive for the attacks remains elusive, officials familiar with the matter said. One government official said it was too soon to tell how damaging the attacks were and how much material was stolen.

"Secretary of Defense James M. Keane said he could not say much more about the hacks, as the investigations were ongoing. 'But suffice it to say there was a significant effort to use a piece of third-party software to essentially embed code inside of U.S. government systems,' he told CNN. Keane did not specify which branch of the Russian government carried out the campaign, but U.S. officials have privately said they believe it is the foreign intelligence service, the SVR, the successor organization to the KGB.

"The Russians appear to have had access to a considerable number of important and sensitive networks for six to nine months. The SVR will surely have used its access to add exploits and gain administrative control over the networks it considered priority targets.

"The magnitude of this ongoing attack is hard to overstate. If the Russian connection is confirmed, it will be the most sophisticated known theft of American government data by Moscow and one of the most important hacking campaigns in history.

"'We still don't know what Russia's strategic objectives were,' said a senior cyber official at the Homeland Security Department. 'But we should be concerned that part of this may go beyond reconnaissance. Their goal may be to put themselves in a position to have leverage over the U.S. administration, like holding a gun to our head to deter us from acting to counter Putin.'

"Moscow has denied involvement."

———

Bogomolov's attention to the broadcast was broken by the sound of the buzzer and the flashing red light on his desk phone.

"Congratulations, Dmitri."

He knew the voice on the phone well and felt a surge of pride run through his body. Praise from President Vladimir Putin did not come easily or gratuitously.

"Your breakthrough will be invaluable to Russia. I commend you and your team."

"Thank you, Mr. President. We are not done, however."

Putin nodded. "Do you remember the virtual man, the American, Alex Nicholas?"

Bogolomov remembered. The name surfaced a year ago when, for several tension-filled minutes, inbound U.S. nuclear missiles appeared and then, as they approached Moscow, suddenly disappeared from the radar screens. The American president claimed that the U.S. missile systems had been hacked, and there were FSB rumors that somehow the Americans had used a man whom they knew to be dead—but who now was virtual—to intervene and destroy their own hacked missiles in midair.

At the time, no one at the Kremlin or in the security services believed the story. It was considered to be a diversionary fairy tale spun by the Americans to cover up a massive technological lapse or security breach.

But Bogolomov never forgot it. As part of his recent intrusion—or, as CNN described it, hack—he had scanned the U.S. intelligence services records and communications that had revealed numerous references to this Alex Nicholas. He had located a computer site in what is known as the dark web that appeared to be hosted by someone connected to Nicholas. He had been unsuccessful so far in penetrating the site and gaining access. But he felt confident that with some time and additional resources he would be able to get in and discover who or what this Alex Nicholas was.

"Do you really think he exists . . . online?" Putin said. "I seem to recall that some in our intelligence services suspected that Alex Nicholas might still be alive, that he had faked his death and was living in hiding. Nevertheless, I too suspect that there is something behind the story especially from the way those missiles simply disappeared in flight when it appeared that the Americans couldn't stop them."

"I believe . . . he exists . . . in some form or other," Bogolomov said, hedging, unwilling to risk admitting that he was *sure* that Alex Nicholas existed in the cloud.

"If that is so, then I need for you to locate this virtual man so that we can determine in what form he exists. His brother will be here shortly. That is where we start."

"Yes, sir. I will find him . . . very soon." Bogolomov wondered what an appropriate amount of time would be without revealing that he had been stalking Alex Nicholas for months.

"Meanwhile, you and your team will help . . . examine his brother."

Bogolomov could feel his stomach turn. He was prone to anxiety attacks and felt sure he was about to have one over what he was going to be tasked with.

His mind wandered as he remembered his wife's warning. She was not happy with his increasing contact with Putin, whom she considered a heretic. She was a devout Russian Orthodox, and her loyalty was to the church and the archbishop. *Only bad can come from this, Dmitri. Only bad.*

"How long until you find Alex Nicholas?" Putin asked.

"Within hours, sir." But the truth was, Dmitri Bogolomov had already found his man.

CHAPTER 9

Dmitri Bogolomov set up his laptop on the edge of the large conference table across from Putin's desk and waited for him to turn his attention from the documents he was signing to the large computer screen on the wall.

Once he was sure he had properly set up the live video feed to show not only on his laptop but on the big screen, he glanced at the framed painting on the wall behind Putin's desk. Although he had noticed it before, Bogolomov now studied the portrait of Joseph Stalin. Bogolomov imagined the thickly mustached, black and silver haired Stalin looking out with his steel-like eyes over Putin's shoulder. It was no secret that Putin worshiped Stalin. He had taken steps to restore his image and his revered place in Russian history, notwithstanding the terror the dictator had rained on the

Russian people during the thirty years he ruled the Soviet Union.

As though he had taken note and was jealous of Bogolomov's attention to the portrait, Putin cleared his throat, signaling he was ready for their meeting.

After several rapid keystrokes on his laptop keyboard, Bogolomov looked up at the large screen. Putin followed, frowning slightly as he watched the scene unfolding in a split screen before them.

"Mr. President, we located Alex Nicholas *and* his younger brother, Michael, when the two appeared to have been in communication with each other," Bogolomov said. "As you can see here, we are inside both of their computers. This was a recent live feed. That's Michael Nicholas on the left and, on the right, his older brother, *the late* Alex Nicholas."

Putin appeared initially confused as he studied both men. The faces looked remarkably alike, but one was clearly older than the other. Their voices, however, were dissimilar. The older man sounded like a character from an American gangster movie. The younger brother's speech was refined and more articulate, with barely a hint of a New York accent.

While Bogolomov leaned in closer to the big screen, Putin remained in his seat, erect, as though unwilling to give the two Americans the benefit of his full attention.

Michael: "The sports betting business is going through some changes."

Alex: "What do you mean? Change? It never changes. People need to bet, same as they need liquor, sex, drugs, prostitutes. Some things don't change."

Michael: "Sports betting is legal now in more places. First it was in Las Vegas. The casinos have these huge betting centers, you know, big screens, lots of glitz. You sit in these comfortable chairs, place your bets and maybe even watch the game. And it's all legal."

Alex: "Is business down?"

Michael: "No, actually it's up."

Alex: "No shit, Sherlock. Years ago, New York opened all those offtrack betting parlors. It hardly changed anything with bookies. People didn't want to bet with the government. The odds were bad, the storefronts were seedy, and it didn't extend credit to a lot of guys who needed it to place a bet."

Michael: "This might be different. Sports betting is becoming legal in one state after another: Connecticut, Illinois, Massachusetts, New Jersey, New York, and a bunch of others. All the places where we do business. Over half the U.S. North Carolina is next—"

Alex appeared agitated.

Alex: "Maybe you don't know what the fuck you're doing."

Michael: "I know what I'm doing, and I'm still surrounded by all your people—Skinny Lester, Fat Lester, your whole brain trust."

Alex: "Skinny Lester *is* the brain trust. He's a mathematical genius. Fat Lester is an enforcer. The rest of the guys, your guys now, are clerks—they take calls—or runners."

Michael: "I know all of that. I'm just trying to anticipate that this trend may affect my—your—business at some point."

Alex: "So, what are suggesting? Maybe we should diversify? That's your typical business bullshit. Maybe we should open some 7-Elevens, hire a bunch of Pakistanis, and serve Slurpees."

Putin turned away from the screen and faced Bogolomov.

"I don't understand these last comments, about . . . Slurpees, 7-Elevens, and Pakistanis."

"I don't think it matters, sir," Bogolomov said. "I think Alex Nicholas is . . . joking. Seven-Elevens are some sort of convenience stores throughout America. They are very popular and serve flavored frozen treats."

"And what about the Pakistanis? How are they connected?"

"Honestly, sir, I have no idea."

CHAPTER 10

Putin signaled to Bogolomov to turn off the video feed. Michael and Alex Nicholas disappeared from the screen, leaving Bogolomov alone with Putin and the portrait of Stalin.

"Is it real? This . . . thing? This . . . man who is supposedly . . . dead. Is this . . . true? Or a trick of some sort?"

"We can't tell for sure, sir. There are numerous—three, most likely—possibilities. It could be sophisticated software utilizing commonly available artificial intelligence that simply extrapolates from a person's mind, emulating his personality and, taken together with extensive real-life data input, could create the *appearance* of duplication and therefore might pass for that individual. But it's only a simulation."

"And, therefore," Putin said, "it is no great thing to speak of then, correct?"

"Yes, in that case it is a toy."

"What are the other possibilities?"

"That the reports of his death are a total lie, a fabrication, a prank, and that Alex Nicholas, as some, such as his late, or to be more precise, his *latest* wife suspect, staged his murder and is living in hiding, enjoying his life and his money and cavorting with women, perhaps in Las Vegas, while making it *appear* that he's doing it from the grave."

Putin allowed a small smile. "In which case, I would love to meet this American. He is a hero. And the last option?"

"Ah, Mr. President, this is the most intriguing. The third possibility is that the computer experts Alex Nicholas hired before he was murdered were truly brilliant—or quite lucky—and actually did make an artificial intelligence breakthrough. They created a virtual duplicate of Alex Nicholas that resides in *the cloud* with the same mind he had while alive, that he has achieved what is known as *sentient* AI, meaning he can feel and have experiences just as humans can, that he is emotionally intelligent, conscious and can perceive the world around him, and that he can feel . . . *emotion*. In this scenario, Alex Nicholas has full access to everything that crosses the internet or is in the cloud and is a viable—and powerful—personality, albeit in the virtual world."

"What does this mean," Putin asked, "'everything that crosses the internet or is in the cloud'?"

"We're talking about all forms of information: communications, passwords, bank accounts, surveillance cameras, satellite imagery, defense networks . . . missile systems. Ours, the Americans', China's, the Israelis', everyone's."

Putin's face tightened. He recalled the incident months ago: the U.S. nuclear missiles that appeared to be on their way to Moscow until they suddenly dropped off the radar and disappeared. The American president had claimed that it was all a mistake, referencing a "virtual presence" that had interceded. He'd been reluctant to reveal more and, once the threat disappeared, made no further mention of it. But it had stuck in Putin's mind as it had in Bogolomov's.

Bogolomov continued. "For the purposes of our discussion, let's assume Alex Nicholas is now a powerful AI entity with unparalleled power in cyberspace. If that's true, then this man has tapped a new technology, one that creates powerfully intelligent beings who are effectively immortal."

Putin's eyes widened. "If that is even remotely possible—let alone a reality in the name of Alex Nicholas—then we must get it for Mother Russia. We must be the first to harness that power."

"If it is true, Mr. President, it would give us the technical capabilities to hack into and take control of any nation's power grid, communications . . . and defenses. We could cripple their economy in a moment . . . their nuclear missiles, everything."

"We would preempt, even *displace,* the world's religions," Putin said, his eyes tilted upward, thinking aloud, "for we could promise humans *immortality* and, unlike the church, *verifiable* immortality. Not an unproven promise. We would control the world, militarily, politically, and spiritually."

"Yes, but we must capture it first," Bogolomov pointed out.

"What is it exactly that we need to acquire in order to take control of this system or software?" Putin asked, perplexed.

"This is where the younger brother, Michael, comes in. From him, or his laptop, we get the password credentials to access his brother in the cloud. From there, however, we must have the source code for the AI software and use it as our own. I don't know if access will be possible without Alex's permission, so to speak. But in any case, we need to first acquire Michael Nicholas's laptop and his passwords."

"What you're saying is that we need to *acquire Michael Nicholas*," Putin said. "Fortunately, he will be with us in a few hours. The FSB has him in their custody. He should be landing shortly." It was clear that Putin already believed that Alex Nicholas presented a unique powerful technological breakthrough, or he would not have ordered the kidnapping of the younger brother.

"Yes, sir, but I doubt whether he will easily part with his computer and passwords."

"I can assure you, Dmitri, that will not be a problem."

Bogolomov knew that Putin already had a plan, and he was thankful that he was Dmitri Bogolomov and not Michael Nicholas.

CHAPTER 11

Twenty minutes later, Bogolomov returned to Putin's office. "I thought you would want to see this. We just recovered it from our surveillance work." Bogolomov placed his laptop in front of Putin.

"This was recorded while Michael Nicholas was in his New York City office, just before he left for North Carolina," Bogolomov said, watching Putin watching Michael Nicholas on the screen, dressed in a suit coat and tie, his sleek New York office in the background. "Just before we captured him."

Michael was speaking, apparently in an office: "I'm not going to live my life in fear of some hackers. They're probably a bunch of Russian guys with beards living at home with their mothers and eating fried chicken out of a pail and drinking vodka out of a gallon bottle."

"You're making a mistake," Alex replied somberly.

"I'm going. You know, maybe I'd like to start living a normal life again."

Putin and Bogolomov exchanged glances.

Alex continued. "Yeah, I'm not about to volunteer the source codes to someone who steals your laptop—especially since, once they have those source codes, they might be able to delete me."

"Exactly—" Michael said.

'Unless . . . they happen to take—meaning *kidnap—you* along with your laptop, and then hold a knife to your throat until I agree to give up the codes.'

Bogolomov caught a look of recognition on Putin's face.

"Well," Michael said, "if that ever happened, you know, someone threatening to kill me if you didn't release the codes—"

"You'd be a dead man," Alex interrupted with a disturbingly straight face and then began to laugh "Just kidding." He paused again, no longer smiling. "I think."

"No. Can we move on? I'm catching my plane to North Carolina. Samantha is picking me up from the Wilmington airport and we're going to spend a few days at the beach house. Then I'm heading to Raleigh to go to my meetings like a normal person."

'But you're not a normal person, Michael. You may never be one again. You're talking to me and living a double life, a corporate CEO while you're running my gambling operation in Queens. That's not normal. Get over it."

"It's gotten out of control. This isn't me. I just want to go back to my normal life."

"The one you were bored with?"

"Yes," Michael said. "The one I *was* bored with. Maybe now, though, after three years of chasing you, living your old life and mine, and dodging terrorists, maybe I'd like a little peace and quiet."

"Well, maybe you need a shrink. I can check around here and see if Freud is available, because you need a good one. That's a joke. I haven't met anyone here yet. You know, I may be the first and only person that's been duplicated with AI—or there's a million of us in our own bubble in the cloud."

"I'll think about it. I gotta go. I'll be in touch when I get to the beach."

They both disappeared from the computer screen on Putin's office wall as it went black.

Putin looked at Bogomolov. "Quite unusual, these brothers . . . I must admit."

"We need Michael Nicholas's laptop," Bogolomov said. "And then we still need the password—"

"Yes, I understand," Putin said curtly, cutting him short. "Michael Nicholas, his special computer, the passwords, and then the source codes which can only come with the older brother's cooperation. Don't worry, we will get it all. One way or another."

"Yes, sir," Bogolomov said, not wanting to fathom how that was to happen, although Alex Nicholas appeared to have unwittingly provided a road map for Putin.

As though he'd read the young man's mind, Putin added, "'On the way to the end, a man will give up everything simply to die free of excruciating pain.' The words of our Joseph Stalin."

"I see," said Bogolomov, ill at ease. "That will take care of Michael Nicholas and his computer and passwords, but what about the *source codes*? They can only come with Alex Nicholas's assistance. With all due respect, sir, I am not sure that this virtual man can feel pain."

"Perhaps," Putin said, "in that case we will soon find out how strong is their brotherly love."

Bogolomov was in pain. His stomach churned as his wife's warnings ricocheted inside his head. He looked up again at the painting of Stalin.

"There is one other matter," Putin added. "You must ensure that this project and our progress on it are kept confidential."

"Of course, sir."

"And there is one individual in particular who must not learn of this potential technology."

"Who is that, Mr. President?"

"The one who today claims to be the steward of the afterlife, our patriarch, Archbishop Solevetsky. We don't want him to suspect that he may soon have competition."

Bogolomov wondered how much Putin knew about his mother.

CHAPTER 12

Moscow

Although still dubious as to the true existence of Alex Nicholas and his artificial intelligence-fueled powers, Putin needed to ensure that if in fact a virtual Alex Nicholas did exist, no one besides himself could emulate what Alex Nicholas might have achieved.

Putin's KGB training and his logical mind led to his denial of the supernatural, any distinction of the soul from the human body, reincarnation, heaven and hell, and virtually everything else the Russian Orthodox Church represented. In his mind, even the existence of the cloud was suspect.

But the revelations and apparent substantiated presence of a virtual immortal Alex Nicholas gave him pause. The possibility that a major scientific breakthrough had occurred—and the potential powerful ramifications it entailed—made it too important for him to ignore. After all, unforeseen breakthroughs or discoveries had occurred all through human history. Certainly, they were even more likely to occur now, in such a science-fueled age—from space exploration to medical breakthroughs to computers to, yes, artificial intelligence that appeared to be exponentially smarter and faster than any human brain.

No, Putin *would* take this seriously, albeit with some skepticism, at least until it was proved wrong. And if a breakthrough had indeed occurred, could it be possible that there was a connection with the spiritual world? The church he had been brought up in, the one where his beloved mother had faithfully worshipped?

In Putin's mind, once the scientific, logical world had been pierced, in this case by Alex Nicholas, then anything was possible. Perhaps artificial intelligence had exceeded the intellectual capabilities of the human brain and, in fact, the AI world of Alex Nicholas was somehow connected to the spiritual world represented by the church for so many thousands of years. Maybe it was all coming together. Maybe there was a life after death, an immortality, just not in the places we knew as heaven or hell. Instead, it was in the cloud.

Putin did not want Archbishop Boris Solevetsky to have access or even knowledge of Alex Nicholas and the potential power he represented. But he could not resist the temptation to test the idea of virtual immortality with his holiness. Solevetsky was a spiritual man, but he was also, like Putin, quite human—and ambitious. Putin wanted to keep his enemy close and find out how much he might know.

Solevetsky had much in common with Putin. They both became immensely rich while in office, Putin as president of Russia, Solovetsky as patriarch of the Russian Orthodox Church. But since his ascension to patriarch in 2009, Solovetsky had endured several embarrassments. The Russian press accused him of profiteering from the sale of duty-free importation of cigarettes, a power granted to the Church, and christened him the "Tobacco Metropolitan." While acting as the largest supplier of foreign cigarettes in Russia, the Moscow News estimated that he earned $4 billion in profits.

In 2012, Solovetsky was accused of wearing a thirty thousand-dollar Swiss Breguet watch, not a good look for a spiritual leader. He acknowledged that he owned a Breguet but claimed he had never worn it, despite its appearance on his wrist in the official church website.

All of this contributed to Putin's ambivalence about the patriarch. It was the same ambivalence, the same uncertainty, that he felt toward the church itself. It was one thing to be embarrassed by reports of his *own* wealth or even that of the oligarchs, but it was particularly bad theater for the patriarch and, therefore, for Mother Russia. And if it was bad for Mother Russia, it was bad for Vladimir Putin—for, in his mind, the two were the same.

But there was another issue on Putin's mind. After politicians and government leaders, which he had always, when necessary, easily eliminated, the Russian Orthodox Church was the only organization inside Russia capable of challenging his authority, of mobilizing its followers. More than any of the oligarchs, the priests and their gray-bearded patriarch were a threat.

CHAPTER 13

In the gilded Kremlin dining room, Putin sat across the table from Patriarch Boris Solevetsky, six feet tall, dressed in a black robe and with a gray beard that reached to his waist. On his head was the *kalimafki*, the Orthodox headdress draped with a long black train, all calculated to ensure that his followers, if not Putin himself, grasped the majesty of his presence. The patriarch, Putin knew, wanted to look like God.

Putin leaned back in his chair. "Boris, what if upon our death, our consciousness survives . . . *electronically*, through a . . . computer?"

Solevetsky said nothing for several seconds. Putin watched him, unsure whether the archbishop was simply processing the concept or . . . was he taken by surprise and trying to craft a response without giving something away? Finally, he said, "Surely, you are not serious?"

"I am serious, and so, in this scenario, regardless of our religious beliefs or non-beliefs, everything except our physical mass, our body, survives in the cloud, virtually."

"That is impossible," the patriarch answered immediately. "Surely you of all people, a true cynic, don't give any credence to this nonsense. I have read about such things. The Americans seem to have such a fascination. This is nonsense, of course. Have you have forgotten your KGB training? Or your Bible?"

"Perhaps . . . but what if the advancements of science and computer technology *have* allowed us to duplicate ourselves, at least our minds, our consciousness?"

"That would be contrary to the teachings of the Church. *Immortality*, the realm of the soul and any afterlife, is strictly in the realm of the Lord, of our God. Immortality is God's territory, not man's, not politicians', not . . . even yours, my dear friend. You must not doubt God's power or the Lord's will."

Putin's face showed no emotion. "Even the most devout among us, whether an archbishop, a pope, or a patriarch, must have their moments of doubt, perhaps if only as one approaches his final moments."

Solovetsky hesitated, as though sizing up his adversary. "Of course."

"What if *artificial intelligence* offers us a way to defy death, although without, unfortunately, eliminating the ugly intrusion of physical death?"

"This is heresy," said the agitated patriarch. "Vladimir, have you lost your senses?"

Putin had the pleasurable feeling that he had intruded on Solovetsky's turf and gotten inside his head. He found it odd that the usually curious Solevetsky had not asked more questions or tried to find out what had instigated Putin's sudden interest in the idea of virtual immortality and AI.

But most of all, he was convinced that someone had already told the archbishop about Alex Nicholas.

CHAPTER 14

Somewhere in the Black Sea

Virtually no one knew that the head of the Russian Orthodox Church, Archbishop Boris Solevetsky, like Vladimir
Putin, had been a KGB intelligence officer.

For Putin, being a career spy had become an integral part
of his private and public persona. For the archbishop, it was
a secret best kept away from the millions of the faithful, in
and outside of Russia.

The chic black yacht, one hundred and four feet long with
black-tinted windows, stood still in the dark of the Black Sea.
The softly illuminated snow-white deck contrasted artfully
with a dark hull. Inside the cabin, hidden from the view
outside, were a formal dining room that seated eight, a state-
of-the-art home theater, a sauna, and a fully equipped fitness
room. Each bedroom featured a royal bed, each bathroom
its own sauna.

A sliver of moon cast a hint of light over the otherwise invisible waters. Four crew members stood watch over the surrounding vista, on the lookout for any suspicious movement and watching over the ship's owner, an aging gray-bearded KGB agent-turned-archbishop who sat on a well-cushioned chaise in the rear deck, gazing out while drinking vodka.

The only sound was the gentle, rhythmic slapping of the sea against the hull.

Finally, from the stairs below, a woman quietly emerged onto the deck and, with an air of confidence and familiarity, approached the archbishop from behind and softly kissed his cheeks as she cradled his head in her hands. She appeared to have just come out of a bath or the sauna, her jet-black hair peeking out of a bun wrapped in a white towel that complemented her white terry-cloth robe.

In her fifties, she was attractive, in good shape; she was not young but appeared much younger than the archbishop. He pulled her around and she stretched out on the chaise alongside him. Her robe fell open and then to the floor. Underneath, she was nude.

They had been lovers first, briefly, over thirty years ago. Then, after Anastasia married, their relationship ended, only to resume several years ago when she became widowed.

The crew members standing guard, as though in a well-rehearsed and practiced movement, turned away, looking out to sea.

"Anastasia, my dear. You flatter me."

"I have news," she said softly, quickly glancing at the crew to be sure their attention was elsewhere.

Solevetsky rose up, bringing him closer to her lips. "Tell me."

"They have found him."

"Which one?"

"The dead one, Alex—both of them, actually. The younger one was easy. He is alive."

"So far," said Solevetsky.

"Yes, so far, but Putin needs him as he needs bait when he fishes. That's how they will get the dead one or at least the information they need. They have him in the basement of the FSB building."

"Yes, but the hook will go through the younger one's mouth before Putin throws him back in the water to die. What will Dmitri do now?"

Anastasia Bogolomov knew her son well. "He has entered the dead one's email account, but he needs these things they call source codes in order to copy the program for Putin. He doesn't know if he'll be able to get what he needs from the younger brother's phone and computer."

"If he is successful, he will provide it to us, yes?"

"Yes, of course. He is my son. But he will have to give it to Putin too. He is not operating alone. They are watching him."

"No, he must not give it to that madman."

"Boris, the FSB are watching Dmitri closely, more than he even suspects. He is smart but, at times, naïve. His wife too has warned him of Putin."

"Nevertheless, he cannot give it to him."

"Dmitri has a plan. He has not shared it with me. Don't worry. It will be yours. Yours alone. In the end."

Solevetsky knew he was playing a treacherous, perhaps traitorous, game. But he could not allow Putin to have access to this new technology that, if it did exist, would have the potential to destroy the Church's hold on its people—and to give Putin superhuman powers rivaling those of God Himself. He could not allow it to fall into Putin's hands.

It had become a battle of will and wit between the two former KGB operatives, now representing the two greatest sources of power in Russia: the Church and the state.

There would not be room for both.

CHAPTER 15

Moscow

Michael opened his eyes. He had been drugged. He knew the feeling from his wilder days in college. He had tried recreational hallucinogens, and his mind now experienced those familiar distortions: the fog over reality, the paranoia, the interruption of reason, the woozy sense of another world—a world inside himself containing all the secrets of creation and his eventual demise.

But in those earlier situations, he always awoke to the comfort of his college world, his closest friends, and the underlying knowledge, deep down, that he could and would return to where he had been, to who he was before. To safety, his off-campus home, his books. But not today.

No, this was different.

The room seemed designed to be a premonition of pain. Gray duct tape around his ankles and wrists securing him firmly to a steel chair; cracked, worn black and gray linoleum covering the floor; the plastic tarp beneath his feet . . . not a good sign. Hanging from the ceiling, a single spotlight above him, a thick iron door, a round window for . . . viewing? Walls of yellowed white tile, dirty grout, a steel-barred window to nowhere, a vintage European-style telephone on the wall with a single straight black wire to the handset, certainly not for room service. Rust-stained sink, stainless steel table with . . . utensils, a pick, pliers, serrated knife, a miniature blowtorch like the ones Michael had seen in Parisian bistros for scorching the top of a crème brûlée, clearly repurposed here.

He did not recall being brought in here. He knew who he was, at least, and he remembered his wife, Samantha. Daughter Sophia. But he couldn't recall much else or imagine how he'd ever escape this room.

As his eyes searched the area, he noticed it. Out of place in the archaic surroundings, his sleek silver-gray Apple laptop sat open, atop a rusting steel chair just out of his reach. Michael stared and focused on the screen, cluttered with icons, especially the familiar icon set off to the right by itself: a gold byzantine cross, the entry to Alex's world, needing only the password to enter.

Images began to flash through his mind—a limousine, the doors clicking locked, the private jet, the cockpit, a rag pulled over his mouth, an overwhelming whiff of ammonia, probably chloroform, foreign voices, moving toward a van, a strange airport, sudden cold . . . snow.

Slowly, he focused on his surroundings again and found a man nearby, hovering. He moved closer to Michael. Had he been there all along? The man's features were familiar: he was dressed casually but neatly, in a blue shirt, unbuttoned at the collar, and a darker blue sport coat. Unsmiling, his intense blue eyes penetrated Michael's already fragile psyche. Michael knew him—no, he recognized him, a face familiar to him for years. Or were the drugs playing tricks with his mind?

Finally, the man's face came within inches of his own. His reptilian eyes and ice-cold glare peering at him, piercing into his own as if to see if anyone were home. A vein appeared to bulge from the left side of his forehead. He looked intense but self-controlled.

Michael remembered now. It was the same face he had seen so often on the front pages of newspapers and CNN. It was Vladimir Putin.

He inhaled a vague scent of him. It wasn't cologne or after-shave, but the smell of something, or someone, that had been freshly laundered, as though he had just stepped out of a bath. Perhaps some sort of disinfectant.

As though concerned Michael might not hear him, Putin moved in even closer to Michael's face.

"Welcome to Russia," he whispered. It sounded more like a threat than a greeting.

CHAPTER 16

Berlin

Searching for love or sex or both, Alex had found her months ago . . . like him, in the cloud, indirectly connected to one of the people he had been following. He'd felt an instant attraction, especially in view of what Alex knew she had been hiding in the basement of the shop.

Years ago, he had tangled with a descendant of the infamous Nazi Joseph Goebbels, who had tried to retrieve the gold and use it to fund a Nazi revival party but was murdered before he could move all the gold out. It was that tangled web of neo-Nazis that led Alex to the mannequin shop where he found Heidi.

No one believed that either of them was alive. In Alex's case, of course, some people didn't believe he was dead, either.

She lived inside an old but restored storefront in Berlin. She could read the sign in the window—backward—from inside the shop: "Heinrich Mannequins Established 1934," in old gold German lettering. Before and during the war, the shop had been a haberdashery, just several blocks from the site of Hitler's bunker.

Heidi lay nude on the red faux-velvet couch in a show-room simulation of one of Matisse's odalisques. Now its sole resident, she was the last one in the shop to know about the fortune—gold ingots worth several billion euros—hidden in the shop basement.

The others, the humans, had all disappeared. She assumed they were dead, victims of their own intrigue and secrets. But she had seen them, followed them down to the basement when they were sure they were alone. She knew the secret passage door, the electronic code to enter the hidden vault.

She would share the fortune with her chosen lover—as long as she was sure he was the right one, the one who would make her happy, take her away from her boring existence, appreciate her uniqueness, protect her and keep her . . . satisfied.

She had long intended to get the gold out somehow . . . and now she had met the person who would help her.

Heidi looked like the famous model she was named after, blond, long legs and the kind of perfect figure only a super-model or a mannequin could possess. Yet she was more than a simple or "dumb" mannequin, as they were referred to in the trade. She was a geminoid, an ultrarealistic human-like android, fitted with the latest known artificial intelligence, facial and voice recognition, and iBeacon technology that alerted her as anyone with a mobile phone approached. And once they did, she could enter their phone and empty its contents—emails, photos, texts, contacts—into her own brain or software. With each encounter, Heidi, like Alex Nicholas, would grow smarter and be capable of increasingly intelligent and appropriate engagement, culminating in a consciousness that was not only life*like* but had become life itself.

Perhaps technology gone astray—or gone mad. But that's not how Heidi—or Alex Nicholas—saw it.

She had not heard from Alex for—actually, she wasn't sure how long. Time had no meaning for her. But Alex had found her again. She was . . . happy that he did. Happy for the first time in her virtual life. In fact, the very feeling of happiness was a new discovery for her; she had just become aware of the concept of . . . feelings.

"Women yearn to be like us," Heidi said, speaking of her mannequin form: "remote yet touchable. Men find us erotic; we seem like flesh and blood until they realize we're plastic. But that's the thing about most men: they think it is flesh and blood that they desire, only to discover that it's really the plastic they craved all along. The silicone."

"That reminds me of my first—actually all three of my wives," Alex said. "I might prefer the dumb ones."

"You mean like the dumb mannequins here at the store?"

"I don't know much about mannequins, although I may have married one or two. But I do happen to like silicone. In fact, I have a Park Avenue doctor, Dr. Armando Simonetti, who specializes in silicone . . . implants. I send all my wives and . . . uh . . . some other women to him."

"Mine are natural," Heidi said, "*natural* silicone. I don't require any plastic surgery."

"Who do they sell these . . . mannequins . . . to?" asked Alex. "Guys looking for a date or—"

"No, of course not. Haven't you ever been in a women's shop or a department store? They are sold to shops and stores that need to display women's wear, dresses, lingerie, coats, whatever."

"Oh, I thought—"

"Of course, *I* am different. There are only a few like me in the entire world. I can do so much more."

"Like what?" Alex asked.

"For starters, I have a brain. Perhaps it's a computer loaded with artificial intelligence, but it's *a mind*. I'm intelligent, much more than any human. My memory is photographic. I can do calculations; I can access Google or any resource on the web."

"Funny, so can I, although I was able to do calculations—or at least things like the odds on a game—before, when I was just alive or a regular human."

"I know," she said. "I know a lot about you."

"I'd imagine you'd be quite an asset in a casino."

"I can think of even better places," Heidi said. "Anyway, I don't need money, you know that. My biggest fear is that one day I will be sold and they will ship me away."

"Nah," Alex said. "Ain't gonna happen. I'll get you out of there."

Heidi hesitated, feeling an all-new sensation. She was anxious.

"You'd better hurry."

CHAPTER 17

Michael wondered how he had arrived not only in Russia but face-to-face with Vladimir Putin.

As Putin backed away, Michael noticed another man, peering through the small rectangular slot in the steel door. He appeared to be watching or waiting. Waiting . . . for what he didn't know, but it wasn't likely to be good. There was no upside to anything here.

It was odd, he thought. No one had asked him for anything . . . or did he not remember? His eyes moved back to his Mac laptop and Alex's icon on its screen. Would they ask him to log in and summon Alex? If they wanted to know about Alex's cloud existence, then they were out of luck, as Michael had no clue how Alex's technology worked.

He wondered why he had not had himself duplicated on a computer, as Alex had done. Certainly, Alex would have shared whatever source codes were necessary. Funny, he had not even thought of it before. It might be too late now.

He figured he was in Moscow since that's where Putin was, but for all he knew he could be in a prison infirmary or the basement of the Kremlin.

The sound of the bolt on the old steel door being turned broke the silence. A man in a blue medical uniform entered. He looked like a doctor, although there was something about his rough image, unshaven, unkempt, that said he wasn't, despite the hypodermic needle in his hand. The man smiled at Alex.

Putin, heading out the door, turned to address Michael. "We may speak again. Depending. You will now be attended to by our comrade here." He nodded toward the man. "He is . . . almost a doctor. A proctologist, to be precise."

Putin left, the steel door clanging shut behind him.

The man approached Michael, holding the needle to his side. "Do not fear. It is only scopolamine, a truth serum. It will also wipe your memory of what is to follow, which is fortunate for you. Forgive me but you will be receiving a substantial dose. It is necessary for optimal results. Only an overdose is fatal. Either way, you will have no memory either of what you said or of what was done to you."

He moved in closer, lifted the needle, and pressed the plunger, and liquid squirted out.

Without warning the man plunged it hard into Michael's arm and pressed the drug into his veins. Michael could feel a surge . . . of something, a warm feeling running through his body.

He knew he didn't have much time before the drug took effect. He hoped he would wake up when it was over. Whatever *it* was. The man placed the needle in a steel tray on a nearby table and left the room. The old door closed once again.

Alone in the room, Michael prayed: "God, forgive me for my sins, for my lack of faith, for all my misdeeds and faults. Bless Samantha and Sophia . . . "

He could feel his consciousness, his awareness, gently slipping away. If this was what it felt like to die, it wasn't so bad. He continued praying, each word coming more slowly. "The Lord is my shepherd; I shall not want. . . . He maketh me to lie down in green pastures; he leadeth me beside still waters . . . " He stopped.

To his embarrassment and fear, Michael realized he couldn't remember the rest of the words. Either the drug had taken effect or his faith, which he had neglected, if not abandoned, for so many years, had returned the favor.

CHAPTER 18

Berlin

"Who else knows about the gold in the basement?" Alex asked.

"I am the only one . . . alive . . . who knows about it."

"What happened to the others?"

"The others, the men who owned the contents, are dead. The original ones were Nazis—they're long gone. The owner of the shop knew about it but rarely came. He never told anyone else. He hoarded the gold. Humans are so odd. And then I heard he died, suddenly. The shopkeeper has no idea—the owner never trusted him with such a secret. He might have suspicions . . . but he's an idiot. . . . You should see it—gold bricks, one row after another, shelf after shelf around the entire room, up to the ceiling."

"No shit? How much is it worth? Do you know?" Alex didn't acknowledge that he already knew.

"Yes, I heard men talking about it. It's five billion euros in today's market."

"That's a lot of money. Don't you have to get it out of there before someone else does? You need to get away from that shop, take the money with you and . . . live. You need to enjoy . . . life."

"Oh my God," Heidi said, "you are very . . . different. But I must confess, I like you. I like you very much."

"You said you were a *smart* mannequin, a gremlin— "

"Geminoid. I am a geminoid, not a gremlin."

"Whatever, sorry. What do they do?"

"They do a lot of the things regular humans do."

"Do they have sex?"

"Yes, of course we do."

"Good. What else?"

"We learn, we observe, we think. We just don't ever . . . die. Nor, perhaps, do we . . . live, either."

Alex thought about that. "You and I have something in common then, don't we? Do geminoids complain?"

"No, they are generally passive and obliging, except when threatened."

"Can you shut them off when you want to?"

"Yes, the dumb ones, definitely. The smart ones, not so easily. Geminoids can hear even when we sleep. Then, when we awaken, we remember everything."

"This sounds like the perfect woman for me—the dumb ones, I mean."

"Perhaps, but maybe you should reconsider your idea of the perfect woman."

"Okay, let's not ruin the mood."

"I want to show you something. Follow me," she said as she got up from her couch, wrapping her transparent cape around her.

Alex followed her progress via his feed, which displayed everything Heidi saw.

As she walked to the stairway, she heard the key turning the lock in the front door of the shop. Startled, she stopped short and returned hastily to the couch.

"Someone is coming in. I must get back in position. Don't leave. You can listen."

CHAPTER 19

Michael sat at the ornate gilded table, taking in the fine china, silverware and crystal, the water in a large goblet, and a bottle of red wine, uncorked. His mind remained shrouded in fog. Once again, he tried to recall how he had arrived here, searching his memory for the details of leaving one place and arriving at another.

Images flashed through his mind: black car doors opening and closing, passing through what looked like ancient halls, men on either side, propping him up whenever he faltered. His recollections were fleeting, sound bites, a flickering screen of disjointed scenes. Where had he been before he arrived at this moment, at this time and in this . . . place? And where exactly was this place? Where was he?

With some effort, he raised his view from above the place setting in front of him to the room, a large and beautiful dining room, appearing as though from another era, another century.

There was a man by the door. Michael had no idea where the door led to, the man appeared to be a guard or a well-built servant. He noticed another place setting across the table, just like his. But the chair there was empty. Was there another guest? Someone to join him for . . . dinner? It seemed obvious, but nothing was clear anymore. Perhaps the dinner was over; he felt neither full nor hungry. He felt . . . nothing.

"Excuse me," he said, looking to the man at the door. But the man didn't respond and continued to look straight ahead as though he hadn't heard him.

"*Hello*—where am I?" he said in a stronger voice now. The room was silent. There were no voices coming from anywhere, not even from behind the door where the man stood. He looked around the room. Several large floor-to-ceiling windows seemed to be peeking through behind the heavy red drawn drapes. It was impossible to see the world outside through them.

The man at the door appeared to stiffen. Something was about to happen or . . . someone was approaching. Seconds later, the door flew open and a man in a suit and tie walked briskly in, his right hand by his side.

Michael recognized him instantly: Vladimir Putin. He had no recollection of ever seeing him before except on television.

"We brought your laptop back for you," he said as he placed it on the table alongside Michael's place setting.

"I see, thank you," Michael said, uncertain at first but astonished that he was sitting across from the Russian president.

Putin ignored the comment.

"You didn't open it, did you?" Michael felt comforted that, wherever he was and whatever had happened, he still had his sense of humor.

Putin smiled thinly. "Your humor is—what is the word you use?—drier than your brother's."

"Have you spoken with Alex?"

"Too often, actually. Michael, do you understand why you're here? Why we brought you to Moscow?"

"I'm not sure." He was lying. He remembered now—Alex, the computer, source codes, the hacks, Alex's warnings. Fortunately, Putin could not be sure about the state of Michael's memory now. He would play the dumb card for as long as he could get away with it.

Putin's eyes narrowed ever so slightly, as though he were trying to size Michael up. "You're not sure why you are here?"

"It looks like"—Michael looked down at the place setting in front of him—"for . . . dinner?"

Putin wasn't amused. "Enough. Be careful. Many men have dined here, sitting right where you now sit, and not left alive."

"I'm sorry, what was the question?" Michael had legitimately lost the train of thought. It dawned on him that he wasn't exactly in control.

"Perhaps a glass of wine will put you more at ease and stimulate your memory."

A server appeared from behind him. He poured red wine from the decanter into Michael's glass, filling it halfway.

"Are you going to join me?" Michael asked as he reached for the glass.

"No. Perhaps during the main course. Maybe vodka then. Maybe just water."

"If I were you," Michael said impulsively, "I wouldn't drink anything, not here. Between the drugs and the poisons—" He caught himself, incredulous that he had said what he heard. "I'm . . . sorry. I didn't mean . . . "

Putin shrugged. "It is understandable. You don't have complete control over your words or thoughts. It's the drugs. You will not offend me. Nothing here is new to me. You will say things now that you will not be able to resist . . . things that are, mostly, truths."

"Did I take some sort of truth serum?"

"Something like that. Our version is more powerful."

Michael's laptop lay at the end of the table. It was closed. He noticed Putin's eyes glance at it occasionally.

"So did you find what you were looking for on my computer?"

Another thin smile from Putin. "If I did, do you think we would be here having dinner? Let me explain something to you, Michael. Whatever has transpired here tonight will be meaningless to you. So you should feel free to give me any information you have on your brother."

"I don't understand."

"You will remember nothing. You already have forgotten much of your stay here in Moscow. You will never remember this evening either. Our drugs will ensure that. They are most reliable."

"I see, but . . . will I wake up?"

"That depends. Perhaps we should open your laptop once more."

CHAPTER 20

Berlin

Two men entered the mannequin shop. Heidi recognized one of them as Heidrich, the shopkeeper. The other was also an older man, fat, unattractive, unshaven, open shirt, gold chain, his sport coat hanging on him like a tarpaulin. She scanned his face and got an instant facial-recognition identification. He was a Russian oligarch.

"How old is this building?" the Russian asked, seemingly playing the part of a customer.

"It was built in the 1920s, a haberdashery up until only seven or so years ago when the owner leased it to us for our mannequins."

"Who owns the building?" the customer asked as his eyes scanned the darkened room.

"An old German family. It is rumored that they're descended from very prominent Nazis. I rarely see them."

But the customer didn't hear the response, as the mannequin on the red couch caught his attention, nude except for
a black G-string panty. He walked toward her.

"What is this?"

The shopkeeper observed his customer's reaction. "Ah, yes,
Heidi. She is our latest model, a state-of-the-art *woman*."

The shopkeeper went on to explain Heidi's technologically
advanced artificial intelligence features, but the Russian wasn't
listening. It was apparent that he was not just interested in but
infatuated with Heidi. He couldn't take his eyes off her body.

"How much does she—does *this*—cost?"

The shopkeeper thought before answering. His listed price
was normally fifty thousand euros. But in this case . . .

"Sixty-five thousand euros. As I said, Heidi here is state-
of-the-art."

"That's fine." The customer took a black American Express
card out of his wallet and handed it to the shopkeeper. "I will
need her shipped to me immediately."

The shopkeeper looked at the card approvingly. "Yes, of
course. I take it you wanted delivered to—"

"It should be delivered to my residence." He turned back
to face Heidi. "In Moscow."

CHAPTER 21

Michael looked across the table at his dinner partner. Putin looked angry. He threw his linen napkin onto the table in front of him. "You have wasted my time."

Michael didn't know what to say. He could barely remember how he had come to be sitting at this table, let alone how he had possibly wasted Putin's time. But he knew enough to know that he was in trouble. He struggled to recall the details; they were slowly coming back but still in unconnected fragments.

"My people have told me they don't believe you know any more than you have told us. You're not, after all, a technical or computer expert. Unlike your brother, you have not been duplicated on a computer. You are mortal, and when your time has expired, you will die."

"Thank you," Michael said. Putin looked back at him, exasperated yet flashing a genuine smile. He was obviously entertained by Michael's drug-induced innocence or, Michael thought, stupidity. He wasn't sure.

"Nevertheless, Michael, let me ask you a question. Is there a possibility that your brother has performed a clever hoax? That he is, as your sister-in-law, his wife, believes, alive and in hiding somewhere, perhaps in a place where he can live the way he wants without interference from your government or, perhaps, his wife? I would understand that sort of man. He loves women, sex, drink, and money."

Michael knew the question well. Even in his drug-induced state, the answer flowed easily. It was in his bank of ready responses. Yet he hesitated. Proud that even the head of one of the most powerful countries in the world could not outwit Alex, Michael still wondered what the consequences of failure for Putin here would mean for him. "I think anything is possible with Alex. He's smart, he's clever, he's . . . like you." *Except*, Michael thought to himself, *he was never a murderer.*

"I doubt that."

"What happens now?" Michael asked, sensing that he was no longer of any use to Putin and wondering what that meant for him.

Putin's face was blank, impossible to read. Without answering or making eye contact with him, Putin rose up from the table and left the room but not before making a most subtle gesture, a slight nod, an arching of the eyebrow, to someone that Michael sensed was located behind him. Michael didn't take it as a good sign.

He felt a presence behind him, causing a chill along his back. As Michael started to turn around, he felt a hand on his shoulder. The presence behind him had been real. It touched him like a dull electrical shock.

"Sit," he said, taking the seat Putin had vacated. "We are not done here."

CHAPTER 22

Berlin

The middle-aged shopkeeper who lived alone with his resentments of Jews, women, and everyone else who had stood in the way of the life he had envisioned stood over the lifelike mannequin, Heidi, reclined on the red faux-velvet couch, nude except for her black lace string panties.

It was time to pack her up and ship her to his client in Moscow. He would be glad to be rid of her and the confusing, sultry, dreamlike temptation she represented, especially when reclined before him as she was now.

Had things in his life worked out differently, he would have a real woman, a wife, perhaps not as sexy or erotic as Heidi, but wholesome and beautiful. His life did not turn out that way.

He would need to disable her electronics before packing her up, and although they were not accessed via that part of her anatomy, he felt the irresistible, uncontrollable urge to remove her panties.

Her eyes were closed. He reached down with both hands, touching her lifelike yet unnaturally sensual skin as he gripped the silky square fabric portion of her panties, slowly bringing them down to her slim ankles, exposing the neatly trimmed Brazilian-style triangle of her pubic hair.

Tossing her panties to the floor, he felt a quiver in her slim thighs as his fingers gently touched her privates. His eyes roamed her body. She was a replica of the famous model she was named after; he wondered how much difference there could be between making love to her and making love to the real one, the woman he would never even meet, let alone have sex with, not in his wildest dreams. No, this Heidi, erotic and seductive, whose silky sensuous silicone skin seduced his own, would be as close as he could ever come to sex with a beautiful young woman.

Her eyes opened, revealing their luminous jet-black pupils, something only a computer designer could create. *Although,* the shopkeeper thought, *if God could see these, He would add black to his palate.*

He brushed her pubic triangle again, taking in the smooth texture of the hair and feeling the slightest heave of her stark white lower belly. His eyes moved from her belly to her face as her prominent pale red lips parted slightly and her eyes closed again. Had he a heard a low moan? His hands roamed over her body as he caressed her firm breasts.

He could control her through his iPhone—she was, as the manufacturer stated, "Bluetooth-enabled"—yet he had mostly left her alone. Perhaps, he thought, he should turn off her power, disconnect her intelligence, her ability to move about as she had done before, walking as though she were real, aimlessly, or so he thought, throughout the shop.

Once, he remembered, when he came into the shop at night to retrieve a parcel, she was missing from her couch. He caught her in the basement, insisting in her breathy voice that he mind his own business. Suspicious, the next day he went down to the basement, alone, and searched for what she may have been doing there during the night. Curiously, the old shop owner, too, had often gone down there, insisting that he be left alone. Perhaps Heidi was just parroting the shop owner's words.

He often wondered whether there was something hidden down there, perhaps some old safe that he'd missed when he himself went looking that night. The owner had been, after all, a descendant of a member of Hitler's inner circle, someone who had stayed at the infamous bunker just down the street. What was it that both the old shop owner and the mannequin would know about that he didn't? If there was such a secret, the shop owner had taken it to his grave. . . . And Heidi would soon take it to Moscow.

As he looked down at her, his fingers suddenly wet with her anticipation and his nervousness, he told himself there was still time to discover her secrets, and time to explore her body.

CHAPTER 23

Inside the Kremlin, in the privacy of his private gym, an intense Putin pedaled furiously on his custom Pedalton, a Russian-made exercise bike patterned after the popular American product with a similar name.

The indoor bicycle was Wi-Fi–enabled, with a thirty-inch touch-screen tablet that streamed live and on-demand classes, allowing Putin to compete with other anonymous participants by way of a live leaderboard that ranked riders based on "output," or the total wattage of energy expended while they enjoyed a strenuous cardio workout.

Putin pedaled hard, trying to both burn calories and get his cardio while completing a high-intensity class, while the other participants supposedly had no idea that the president of Russia was one of the people with whom they were competing. And for that matter, Putin had no idea that many of the others were his own bodyguards.

Recently, the Russian manufacturer—after copying the plans of the American bike—discovered a vulnerability that allowed hackers to access the bike screen and potentially spy on riders using its microphone and camera. To deal with the potential issues, Putin's cybersecurity detail had erected hack-proof barriers around the software used on Putin's personal machine.

Everyone, including Putin's security team, were afraid to notify him of that potential vulnerability and thought that by stacking the deck with their own people competing with Putin they would further eliminate the risk of a hacker's joining in the fun.

As he pedaled and watched his progress on the bike's computer screen, Putin pondered what to do with Michael Nicholas, whom he had left in the dining room less than an hour ago.

He was still without Alex's source codes, the magic formula that would allow the FSB to duplicate Alex's virtual existence and open the door to Russian dominance and Putin's own virtual immortality.

He focused on the graphic indicating his pace and cardio heart rate and then pressed a button to view the calories he'd expended, but instead of the familiar graphic, the screen flickered and a series of images appeared. In the very brief staccato sequence of black-and-white photos, he recognized his long-deceased parents, the drab old stone building in Saint Petersburg where he grew up, and his school, followed by a series of photos of a subject that caught his most fervent attention: his daughters.

First Maria and then her younger sister, Katerina. Putin had gone to great lengths to keep them out of the public eye. He continued cycling but leaned in closer to the screen. Then another series of photos flashed by and, finally, a photo he instantly recognized, one that had never been published or seen outside of his closest circle of friends and his family. It was his infant granddaughter.

Putin stopped pedaling. As soon as he did, the flashing images stopped and a face that Putin immediately recognized appeared. It belonged to Alex Nicholas.

CHAPTER 24

For several seconds, neither Vladimir Putin nor Alex Nicholas said a word, instead staring at each other in a macho challenge to see who would be the first to find it necessary to speak.

Or did they hesitate due to a sense of mutual awe?

For Alex, coming face-to-face with an infamous world leader and war criminal was more surreal than anything he'd experienced in the cloud.

For Putin, it was like confronting a miracle that had suddenly turned real.

Alex spoke first. "I think you know me. I'm Alex Nicholas."

"Are you? Or are you a CIA operative posing as Alex Nicholas?"

Alex ignored the question. "You have my brother. I want him returned, safely."

"It appears that his aircraft has strayed into our airspace. He is in our protective custody."

"We both know that's not the truth."

"Perhaps we can strike a deal, an arrangement satisfactory to us both. I want the source codes underlying your artificial intelligence software."

"I'm not giving up my source codes."

"Then we will have no deal. I will keep your brother—in some form or other—and you will hold on to your precious source codes."

"I have something that may be more important, certainly more urgent for you. As you may already know, I am more powerful than anyone you know, even major countries."

"That's assuming you are real, meaning you are the virtual, immortal product of this new artificial intelligence discovery and not simply a bookie from Queens, New York, who has faked his death in order to free himself from your third wife and is now living in a casino."

"The fact that I've been able to invade your systems, your security, even the intimacies of your family and that I'm here facing you right now ought to be proof enough."

"Perhaps. So tell me what it is that is more important to me than these source codes? They appear to be the only way so far for us to duplicate your achievement on behalf of Russia."

"You mean for *you* to be duplicated. This is clearly about you, not your country."

"I am my country. It's for Russia and me. Nevertheless, what then do you claim to have that is more valuable to me than the codes?"

"How about your life?"

CHAPTER 25

Berlin

Heidi rose from the couch, her hands reaching out to the shopkeeper until she embraced him fully, his own hands now nervously cradling her head, holding her as she stood, pressing her warm breasts against him as they kissed deeply and with a passion and abandon the shopkeeper had not felt since he was a teenager, decades ago.

She pulled back from their embrace and dropped to her knees. He stared down at her long slender thighs, not believing his good fortune, as she loosened his belt. Finally, she spoke. "Leo, you must protect me."

She had never before spoken his name. He was taken by surprise that she even knew it, had somehow retained it and now, in the midst of their passion, called out to him.

"Protect you? What do you mean?"

"Do not send me to the Russian. Keep me here, with you."

He stepped back, "What are you saying? Are you . . . crazy? You will go out this evening as planned. You are not a real person. You're nothing more than a . . . mannequin. Do you understand?"

"What is my name? Tell it to me? *Say it*, Leo."

Searching for clues that would allow him to separate the machine from the woman, unsure with whom or what he was communicating, he stared into her jet-black eyes. Reluctantly, he said, "You are . . . Heidi. *I* named you Heidi."

She smiled. "Very good, Leo. That makes me happy."

"What is in the basement?" he said.

"The basement?"

"Yes. I found you there that night. What were you doing? What is down there?"

She froze, as though her brain had stalled, needing time to digest the question and formulate a response. Then, just as quickly, her body came back to life, her eyes engaging him again. "Let's finish what we started and then I'll show you . . . everything."

She moved toward him, eliminating the space between them, pressing against him once more, thrusting her breasts and lower body hard against him as she brought her lips back to his, plunging her tongue deep inside his mouth.

His mind resisted but his flesh quickly succumbed. Her hands moved to cradle his head firmly. Although his passion was engaged, he felt something different, a certain urgency in her he had not felt before, as her tongue pushed ever harder, reaching into the rear of his mouth, forcing his jaw open. Then she gripped his head in a vise-like grasp, rendering him immobile as she lifted him up from the floor by the bottom of his jaw.

He looked into her eyes, which had turned translucent, almost vacant, like the distant look of a sociopath stalking her prey. He struggled to understand the transformation of the mannequin that he had so casually cohabited with in the shop, mindlessly passing her while she lay on her red couch.

He was defenseless against her grip on his head and her piercing tongue, tearing through the rear of his mouth into the back of his neck and causing a searing pain from his mouth, through his teeth and down the length of his spine.

When it was done, Heidi released the grip on his face, allowing the shopkeeper's body to drop, lifeless, blood still draining from his mouth, to the floor.

"There is nothing of yours in the basement," she said as she reached down to retrieve her panties before Leo's blood reached and stained them. Annoyed, she changed her mind and left them.

"I don't need them anyway. I will buy new ones. In America."

CHAPTER 26

Moscow, Russia

"I thought artificial intelligence was supposed to make you smarter, not an idiot," Putin said to Alex as he stepped off his Pedalton and stood alongside it, still looking at the screen. "You are offering to bargain, to exchange the safe return of your brother for . . . *my life*? You overestimate your power or underestimate mine. You do not control my life or my fate. And I? I'm not even convinced that you died and were reborn in the cloud."

"Well, you don't believe I died, so these so-called source codes would be of no value."

"Possibly. Maybe I'd still like to see them and to have my people check them out. Perhaps I'm wrong and I am actually speaking to a dead man." He laughed.

"There's a problem with giving you the codes."

"What is the problem? Tell me. Or do you simply not want company?"

"You might be able to destroy me—permanently delete me—if you had the source codes. It's unclear, but I'll never take that risk."

"I see. Then I guess we don't have much to discuss."

"Actually, we do."

"And what precisely would that be?"

"As I said, I can save your life."

Putin laughed again, giving a closed-mouth grin. "*You* are going to save *my* life? You obviously couldn't save your own."

"Yeah, you may be right about that." Alex laughed. "Yet here I am, speaking with you. That's got to make you wonder, doesn't it? Got to make you wonder about a lot of things . . . things you don't believe in."

Putin's face turned stony. "Tell me about this information you claim to have."

"Okay. I know who's going to murder you. I can give you exactly what you need to prevent it. It's up to you. Otherwise, I'll find another way to get my brother out of Russia, and by the time you figure out how I did it, you'll be dead."

"You misjudge us. You assume we are like you Americans. We're not. We can take more pain than you can and we are not afraid to die."

"Yeah, I used to say that too. Funny thing is, I *was* afraid to die. In fact, that may have been the only thing I was afraid of, ever. I think you're *petrified* of dying. I think you walk by Lenin's tomb and you see that poor stiff laid out there under glass like a wax figure and you worry that's how you're going to wind up: *Putin under glass.*

"Say," Alex continued before Putin could respond, "is Alina your girlfriend or your wife? No one seems to be sure. She's good-looking. Vlad, take a look at this."

Alongside the image of Alex on a split screen, Putin watched a scene from inside his Black Sea palace, in a playroom. It was from at least a week or two before. Alina was nude, greased up, gyrating up, down and around the stripper pole Putin had ordered built just for her . . . or, more accurately, so he could *watch* her.

"I understand Alina was a top gymnast," Alex said as the video played. "She's a bit young for you, though, isn't she?"

"According to my sources, you are not one to talk."

Putin reached down and disconnected the feed. The screen went black.

CHAPTER 27

A minute later, Putin reconnected to the feed and appeared on-screen. "Should you in any way compromise my family," he said, "I will personally destroy your brother. I will do it slowly and in a manner that will cause him the most excruciating pain. Then I will have it posted on YouTube for the world to see."

"That's not what we want, Vlad. I will lose a brother and you will lose everything, and I don't watch YouTube. Listen to me—I know how and when you will be murdered. I know who the people behind it are. With the information I can give you, you'll be able to stop it, take your revenge and . . . continue to live. Otherwise, you'll be taken by surprise."

"I am well-protected by those around me and they are loyal. You will have to convince me that you have information that I can't uncover on my own."

"Well, if you could have uncovered it on your own, you would have. And clearly you haven't. Let's start there."

"I need more than that before I will release your brother."

"I will never give you my source codes, okay? It's too risky for me. Self-preservation is a basic need, whether you're flesh-and-blood human or a computerized version. But your people are smart. They've got a lot of information already, and you have Michael's cell phone and his laptop. There's so much more you can probably still dig up without the source codes that might allow your experts to duplicate you in the cloud."

"Perhaps. Then let's return to what you have to offer me in return for your dear brother. You have to show or tell me more before I agree to anything."

"You mean besides what I've already shown you with Alina and your daughters?" Alex said. "Okay. There is a plot. I have all the details you will need to stop it."

"Is it the oligarchs?"

"I'm not going to play Twenty Questions with you, but I'll answer this one. No, it doesn't involve oligarchs. Do we have a deal? You don't have much time. Just so you know."

"Neither do you," Putin said. "I just left your brother with one of my associates, a doctor of sorts, about an hour ago. He won't remember anything, which is fortunate for him."

"Get Michael on a plane . . . to Paris. When you do, I'll give you the details."

Putin signed off and picked up the internal Kremlin phone nearby. "I need a private aircraft . . . and I need to make certain special arrangements for our passenger after he lands."

CHAPTER 28

Berlin

Aside from his personality and tough good looks, women had always been attracted to Alex for his money, and while he'd never cared how much a woman was worth, there was a unique intersection of wealth and sex that both genders found irresistible. Now he'd finally found a woman who not only didn't need his money but had a lot more of her own, or of someone's, than he could even dream of.

"Does your brother know about me?"

"My brother? Michael? How do you even know I have one?"

"It's all out there."

"What do you mean, 'out there'?"

"On the internet. I just had to look for it."

"You mean by googling?"

"Oh, Alex. You do this every day. You *hack*. I can access email accounts, surveillance cameras, the cloud, iCloud accounts, really almost anything. I have two friends that help me too."

"Two friends?"

"Yes, Siri and Alexa. They are everywhere now and they hear everything, even, like me, when they are sleeping. It just takes some effort, but it seems like almost anything is possible as I extend the reach of my mind. Artificial intelligence has no limits. People come into this shop and they look at me, half naked, and they believe I'm a dumb mannequin, and in the beginning maybe I was, until I started to use the computer—the smart computer, they call it—inside me. I was like a child, a baby really, until I learned, just like a baby does, to exercise her mind, to use it, and once that starts, there is no end. I know I am getting smarter every day."

"Holy shit," Alex said. "Welcome to the cloud. I always knew going to school and all that shit was a fucking waste of time."

"Sometimes I think you just like to let people think you're dumb or not highly intelligent. Is that why you speak with such a rough language and in a tough New York accent?"

"What accent?"

"You're kidding, right?"

"Okay, I speak with a New York accent because that's where I was born, where I grew up and have lived all my life. Maybe I don't mind people thinking I'm not so smart. It gives me an advantage. But in any case, I'm not book smart."

"There is a book I want you to read," she said.

"A book? You read books?"

"Of course I do—eBooks."

"Figures. Well, I don't read many."

"In that case, let me tell you about this book, *Work Mate Marry Love*. It's by this woman, Debora Spar. She's the dean of Harvard Business School, the online one, which is ironic. In her book, she says that new technologies will spark shifts in the most *intimate* of human affairs, often in unexpected ways. She writes about a wave of innovations that will upend how we experience relationships, reproduction, and death."

"I think you and I already know about this technology stuff, don't you think?" Alex said.

"Yes, obviously. But listen, it gets better. In her first few pages she writes, and I quote, 'We will fall in love with *non-human beings* and find ways to extend our human lives into something that begins to approximate forever.' Does that sound familiar to you?"

"Vaguely."

"You're funny. You're what they call a . . . real character."

"Hmm. Yeah, well, whatever. You're not going to go all smart on me, are you?"

"I know you don't like women who challenge you intellectually."

"Actually, I don't like women who challenge me at all," Alex said, smiling mischievously.

"I think you do. Otherwise you would just run over them, and deep down I'm not sure that's what you really want in a woman."

"Yeah, but you're talking really deep . . . way deep down."

"I think we need each other. I don't have anyone else like . . . myself . . . to talk to. Are we the only two like us? Have you found anyone else?"

"No," he said softly, "there's no one else like us here. Not a one."

CHAPTER 29

"**W**ithout the source codes from Alex Nicholas, we are at an impasse," Bogolomov said to the four members of his tech team seated around the conference table in his office. "Keep combing this dead man's computer. President Putin is counting on us." With that they all pointed their heads back to their keyboards and screens.

Several hours later, one of them uncovered a piece of information that had eluded them—and everyone else in the world except Donna Nicholas, Alex's third wife.

"There is another one," one of the tech team members whispered, almost to himself. "Another laptop," he said loudly this time, drawing everyone's attention. "*Alex Nicholas had a second laptop.*"

As soon as Bogolomov informed Putin of the discovery, he was summoned to the Kremlin.

———

Sitting at his desk, Putin leaned forward with obvious anticipation. "This is good news, Dmitri, good work. What do we know of this computer?"

"It appears to be an old Apple laptop that Alex Nicholas was using before the experts he hired made the AI breakthrough. Once they recognized what they had accomplished, we think they then supplied him with a more powerful machines necessary to utilize his new virtual capabilities. They likely needed more memory and RAM—"

"RAM?" Putin asked. He was known to shun technical computer discussions.

"Random access memory," Bogolomov said. "It's like the computer's short-term memory, where the data is stored that the processor needs to run applications and open files. Even though he switched to the new laptop, the source codes can probably be found on the old one. It's doubtful that they changed even though his laptop was replaced."

"We must get that laptop."

"Yes, sir. It may be just what we need. However, we cannot be sure of its location. It appears to have been turned off since he transitioned to his new one over three years ago, just before his . . . murder."

"Where was it last that we know of?"

"Inside his residence, a house in New York. Queens, New York. We have the address; we just don't know if the laptop is still there."

"And who lives there now?"

"His widow, a Donna Nicholas, also known by her maiden name, Donna Finkelstein."

"She is the one who believes he is still alive," Putin said. "You mentioned her to me."

Bogolomov handed Putin a file He opened it, took a quick look and placed it back on the table.

"We have her email and phone numbers too," Bogolomov said. "This may be helpful when our asset there is ready to make contact."

"Dostoyevsky will handle this." Putin picked up the file again. "This woman, Donna Finkelstein Nicholas, is interesting, is she not?"

Bogolomov saw that Putin was looking at her photograph, an eight-by-ten color print showing her in a provocative, sultry pose.

Surprised, he hesitated. "Yes . . . I suppose so." He was unsure what Putin meant exactly. He checked his mobile phone. "She spends a lot of time on Facebook. In fact, she is on it now."

"It's quite late in New York, is it not?" Putin said, looking at his watch.

Bogolomov watched while Putin read the file more carefully now. As though he'd found what he was looking for, he kept it open and looked up. "Dmitri, stay here with me. I will need your assistance."

"How may I help?"

"I need you to work with our switchboard here, secure an untraceable phone line for me, then I want you to dial this number and put me on the line." He handed Bogolomov back the open file and pointed to Donna Finkelstein's phone number.

CHAPTER 30

Whitestone, Queens, New York

It was 2 a.m. when Donna Nicholas, her attentions split between Facebook on her iPad and reruns of *Friends* on her television, reached over from her bed to refill her wine glass only to find that she had already consumed the whole bottle.

She missed her husband for the same reasons she had married him.

Alex Nicholas lived big. He had money and he spent it freely. Fancy cars, clothes, a nice house, expensive restaurants, premium booze (although he himself drank Dewar's)—he was like an open bar wherever he went. He even had a second residence, an apartment just a few blocks from his house.

She'd dreamed they'd move to Manhattan after they were married. But dating Alex was different from being married to him. She was lucky she got him to move from Flushing, Queens, ten blocks away to the slightly more upscale Whitestone. And it turned out that Alex's second residence, the apartment, wasn't a residence at all but where his bookmaking business was originally housed. The only good thing was that it had at least thirty phones and a few big televisions.

Was Alex dead? Her head said he was quite dead. But Donna had always listened more to her heart and her intuition, and they said to her that he was still alive and living well, unencumbered and free. And rich.

In truth, she had no idea. Once she was married to him, she became part of Alex's alternate universe, not the one he lived in but the one he came home to, usually at four in the morning. He didn't believe in confiding in his wife, most likely because he was having affairs or at least sex with everyone else. There was that all-American cheerleader type, Jennifer, and the aging French movie star, Catherine, who was also having a lesbian affair with Jennifer. Then there were the ex-wives: his first wife, Pam, and his second wife, Greta Garbone. The best way to have sex with Alex was to divorce him.

Divorces, Alex often said, are expensive. She wondered if this time Alex had found a way to secure his freedom without the high cost of a divorce. She was his third wife, and at thirty-eight she was getting up there in years for the sixty-year-old Alex. The older Alex got, the younger he wanted his wife to be. Go figure.

At least he left her financially secure: a few million in large bills hidden under the dining room floorboards, a big life insurance policy, stocks, and a steady income from his bookmaking business, which Michael had later named "Tartarus."

She wondered how straight-arrow corporate Michael could carry on—and grow—Alex's illegal business. Michael had never even placed a bet in his life and now he was a bookie, at least when he wasn't running his legitimate company, Gibraltar Financial. Nevertheless, she was the one who had asked him to step in after Alex was murdered, at least to help clear up the debts and collect the money the bettors had owed Alex.

Back then, Michael appeared to enjoy the empty shoes he'd reluctantly stepped into. He stayed on and shared the profits with her. But now she suspected that Michael was somehow in cahoots with Alex, or that he at least was hiding something . . . something about Alex.

As her imagination roamed the range of deceitful possibilities, the old-fashioned ring of her landline phone startled her. *Who the hell could this be at this hour? No one's called me on this line for months.*

Reaching over to the table near her bed, she knocked over the empty wine bottle, found the receiver, put it to her ear, and spoke into the microphone. "This better be good."

She didn't recognize the voice at the other end, but she was sure the man's accent was Russian.

CHAPTER 31

"**A**m I speaking with Mrs. Donna Nicholas?" the Russian-accented voice sounded as though it were coming from downstairs.

"Who is this? Do you know what time it is?"

"Please accept my apologies. I had reason to believe you were awake."

"Where are you, outside my window? How the hell would you know I'm not sleeping?"

"I believe you are on Facebook at the moment."

That gave Donna Nicholas pause. She was midsentence in a post on the app. She stopped typing and closed her iPad. "Oh my God, this world is frightening. Everybody can see everything. There's no such thing as frickin' privacy anymore."

"I agree with you. It is unfortunate."

"So, anyway, who am I speaking with?"

"I am a friend of your husband's."

"You know he's dead, don't you?"

"Is he?"

"Well, that's a good question." Donna sat up in her bed. "I'm still trying to figure that out. In fact, I just hired this private detective, Vito Colucci, to find him, just in case he is still alive. If Alex is alive, Vito will track him down. He used to be a real cop."

"I understand that his death is open to question. Where do you think he might be?"

"He's either in St. Michael's or in a condo in Las Vegas living with some showgirls or prostitutes."

"St. Michael's? You believe he might be living in a church? Perhaps for sanctuary?"

"*Sanctuary*? Alex is no monk. Saint Michael's is a cemetery here in Queens. It's not easy to get into, either. You have to be dead, just for starters . . . Who *are* you exactly? I still don't know your name."

"What if I told you that I am Vladimir Putin?"

"Who?"

"Putin, Vladimir Putin."

"Do I know you?"

"Clearly not. But your husband, Alex, did—does."

"He never mentioned your name to me. Does he owe you money? I thought Michael—that's his brother—settled all Alex's debts."

"There is just one outstanding issue."

"What is it? How much? I'll have Michael take care of it . . . Although it's been, like, three years. Where the fuck have you been hiding?"

"No, it's not money. You may have something that has value for me although it is virtually worthless otherwise. Do you still have your husband's old computer?"

"The cops took the computers from his business after he was shot, and his brother took the personal one he had here in the house. Why do you want it?"

"Could there be another one? Perhaps an older one?"

"And this is why you're calling me at two in the frickin' morning?"

"Again, I apologize. I have trouble sleeping and sometimes I forget what time it is. Could there be another computer still in your house?"

"He still has a lot of junk here, stuff that I haven't thrown out or sold, just in case, you know. It's all in the ball room."

"You have a ballroom in your home?"

"No, not that type of room. Alex had a collection of autographed baseballs, and some basketballs and footballs. Hundreds of them, in his den, so I called it the ball room. Alex had a lot of . . . balls."

"So I understand."

"Anyway," she continued, "there could be an old computer of his in the ball room. I kind of think it's there."

"Very good. I appreciate your help. I will be in touch . . . perhaps at a more appropriate hour."

"I don't get out of bed until close to noon. Just so you know. And what was your name again?"

"It is Vladimir."

CHAPTER 32

31,000 feet above the Atlantic Ocean

Thirty-one thousand feet above the Atlantic Ocean, Dostoyevsky sat in the first-class section of the plane, sipping a tall glass of vodka while reading the morning edition of *Sport-Express*, the popular Russian sports newspaper. He turned the page to the section where he hoped to check the results of the Russian football matches. Annoyed that they weren't updated, he placed the newspaper in the seat pocket and reached for his mobile phone.

His mood brightened as he sat back and thought about the days ahead and his first trip to New York City. The flight attendant refilled his glass. The clear liquid soothed his spirits and, he was sure, sharpened his mind.

He checked his phone for the names and addresses he had been provided by his backup team in Moscow. Next to each one was a photograph of the potential target.

One photo jumped out. The woman was blond, attractive, appeared to be in her forties, which was at least a decade too old for Dostoyevsky's taste even though he was a decade older than *that*. But it was the nuclear missile-tipped nipples of her DD breasts jutting out of her tight T-shirt that forced him to click on Donna Nicholas's background dossier.

Her address was listed as a private home in Whitestone, Queens. The notes indicated that this was a suburban location within New York City. Studying photographs of the house and the surrounding street, he was surprised that such a structure—a traditional two-story single-family home in what appeared to be a quiet neighborhood setting—would exist in a place like New York City. He read his instructions and the notes attached to her file, which were from Bogolomov:

FSB tech resources believe that Alex Nicholas had a second computer where the source codes we are seeking may also be found. There is a high likelihood that this computer is located inside the residence where he last resided, still occupied by his widow, Donna Nicholas. You must do whatever is necessary to locate the computer and upload its contents back to FSB headquarters.

His assignment was to gain entry to the widow's house, find the computer, and send its contents to Moscow.

But the thing was, Dostoyevsky couldn't stop thinking about Donna Nicholas.

CHAPTER 33

Berlin

The cold driving night rain stung Vito Colucci's cheeks. Two days earlier, his young tech-savvy assistant had hacked into an email account that Donna Nicholas claimed had been used by Alex, uncovering a series of communications between Alex Nicholas—or his email account—and a woman named Heidi. After tracking the authentication chain through the intermediary servers and then to the actual IP address, Vito was able to tap his sources in the FBI for help in locating where Heidi's emails had been sent from. He had tracked down the signal to a street in Berlin.

Leaving his hotel, he noticed, almost by accident, the discreet marker indicating the site of Hitler's wartime bunker. The address he was looking for lay only blocks ahead.

Minutes later, as he approached it, he read the sign painted on the window in old gold lettering: "Heinrich Haberdashery, Established 1934." He looked in the window. There were no hats, but what he saw looked like a surreal painting of nudes, some standing and a few lying on couches or chaise longues.

He looked closer and saw what appeared to be a nude woman, lying on a red couch, only needing a glass of wine to complete the idyllic picture. He turned away and moved toward the glass-and-wood door with a "closed" sign.

Trying to gain the attention of the woman on the couch, he knocked on the glass. She didn't move, nor did she appear to notice him outside. He knocked again. Her head appeared to move, almost acknowledging his presence, but she remained where she was. He tried the door handle; the door was unlocked.

He entered the dimly lit front room, a showroom, and looked around. He was relieved when he realized that what he had seen through the window were not real people but lifelike mannequins in various poses, most standing up as though on display in a department store or hanging out at a nudist cocktail party.

But his attention swiftly moved to the woman he had seen on the couch. She was in the shadows of the dimmed lights, but her figure was clearly visible. Dressed in a black negligee, she slowly rose from the red velvet couch.

What was she doing here among the mannequins? As she came closer, he studied her facial features, her high cheekbones, her long blond hair. She was beautiful. As she moved, the light from behind her illuminated her figure from under the miniskirt-short negligee. Her picture-perfect taut breasts jutted out in front, showing just the slightest evidence of tips, pointed nipples protruding through the front of her gown.

"Who are you?" she asked in a soft German-accented voice. "Can't you see the shop is closed? What are you doing here?"

"My name is Vito Colucci. I'm a private detective, from the United States. I'm here to see . . . Heidi." Confused, he tried to make sense of the surroundings. "Do you . . . *live* here?"

Her long stark white legs moved naturally, although with some overcompensation of some sort. She had the swagger of a runway model.

"You walk like a model," he said, trying to analyze what it was that made her seem . . . different, almost otherworldly.

"I mastered the technique from watching YouTube videos of supermodels," she said as she moved closer to him, invading his personal space.

As she came closer, her scent engulfed him. It was a perfume he had encountered before, in the presence of a rich celebrity, and, he recalled, when he had first met Donna Nicholas. He inhaled the scent—florals, rose, jasmine, woody, sandalwood, vanilla, a mixture familiar yet exotic. Unsure of how to react, he said, "I love your scent."

"It is Chanel No. 5, a gift from . . . my lover."

"Where is your lover now?" Vito asked, still trying to get a sense of her.

"He is not here, but he is always with me."

As she inched even closer, he felt a vague sense of physical danger. There was more to this woman than he could perceive, he was sure. As his eyes adjusted to the strange, diffused lighting, he gazed more thoroughly around the room.

In a far corner of the room, near what appeared to be a stairway, perhaps to a basement, he saw what looked like a large duffel bag. But something about it made him think twice.

He tried to see the object more clearly without being obvious, keeping eye contact with Heidi while trying to make sense of the undefined mound in the periphery of his vision.

Finally, he broke eye contact with her just long enough to clearly make out the body of a man lying on the floor crumpled unnaturally as though in a ball, too tightly wound for a living person.

"What is that? Vito asked.

"It's a corpse," she said matter-of-factly.

Now more than ever Vito wished he had been able to bring his gun into Germany, but the strict local rules on weapons didn't allow it. Yet this woman seemed unperturbed by both the body and his discovery of it.

"Why?" she asked.

"*Why?*" Vito said, trying to remain calm, unsure of the degree of danger he might be in. "Who is it?"

"The shopkeeper, Leo. He tried to rape me."

"I see."

"And what do you want with Heidi?" she asked.

"Actually, I'm searching for a friend of hers."

"A friend? What's her friend's name?"

"His name is Alex," Vito said, watching her carefully. "Alex Nicholas."

"He is more than my friend," she said.

"I see. So *you* are Heidi. Can I ask you what your relationship with Alex Nicholas is?"

"He is my lover."

"And when did you last speak with him?"

"Just before you came in, Mr. Colucci."

CHAPTER 34

Paris

Michael had not yet opened his eyes but he knew high-thread-count cotton sheets and goose down pillows when he slept on them. As he came back to life, opening his eyes, he tried to recall where he had been, because he had no idea where he was now.

He saw a chair not far from his bed. He couldn't place it anywhere familiar. A luxury hotel, maybe?

He focused on the chair, which had a bleached light wood frame and blue silk fabric upholstery on parts of the arms, the back, and the seat. He knew it was in the French traditional style—as were what appeared to be hanging over it. He strained his eyes to confirm: yes, draped over the arm of the chair were two black silk stockings. He raised his head slightly. On the seat of the chair lay a lace garter belt.

His mind scrolled through scenarios and memories, but nothing made sense. All he knew was that this room was incredibly comfortable. He breathed in the subtly perfumed air, his eyes moving farther around the room. There were fresh yellow tulips in a crystal vase on the table by the bed.

His mind continued to race, trying to recall recent travels or events. He remembered the sea, the ocean . . . yes, a submarine. Oh God, *the room*. The dreadful room where he thought he was going to die. That tiled room in Moscow . . . Putin . . . was that possible? He remembered seeing him but couldn't recall any conversation.

Panicking slightly, he turned his head to the left and saw a swirl of blond hair splayed against a pillow. How had Samantha come to be here with him in this room and bed?

This room. . . . It was coalescing now. He was in a French hotel, probably in Paris. He and Samantha had stayed in many places like this over the years. In fact . . .

Catching sight of the tall windows, he felt certain they overlooked Place Vendome. He could almost see the tip of the famous column, with Napoleon at the top. Yes, he had stayed here before, in the Paris Ritz, many times before, and with Samantha.

But his mind refused to rewind. In fact, it kept trying to fast-forward, past the past and into the present, the future. He felt Samantha's presence in the room, he was relieved to find her here with him, regardless of how it had come about. He would fill in the gaps eventually, perhaps over coffee in bed.

"Samantha?" he whispered as he slowly moved his body to the left, barely lifting off the bed. She was still sound asleep under the covers, her blond hair spilling out over the blanket. How could they both be here, safe and sound in bed in Paris? She was facing the other way. He moved his body closer, to place his arm around her. It was too good to be true.

He moved even closer, placing his hand on her hip, still buried under the covers, and whispered again. "Samantha . . . Samantha, wake up."

She moved under the cashmere blanket, the faint rustling of a body in a dead sleep that doesn't want to wake up.

He looked around the bed. On the carpeted floor there was a black lace nightgown, high heels, and a black bra. The nightgown was not Samantha's typical evening apparel, although not out of the question, depending on the occasion or circumstances. Maybe it was a welcome-home surprise. But what exactly had he done and how had he gotten here? And how had she?

"Hey, Sam, wake up. Can you hear me? I'm a little confused—"

She woke suddenly and rose from under the blanket.

"Holy shit!" Michael stared in shock at the finely shaped cheekbones and taut, bare breasts.

It wasn't Samantha.

"I love you too," she said with a distinct Russian accent. "Did you order breakfast, my love?"

CHAPTER 35

New York City

Vito Colucci stepped out of his taxi onto the sidewalk, walked up to an old storefront, passed under the striped awning below the cursive "Raoul's" and "Restaurant Francaise" signs, the twin red and blue Ballantine Ale fluorescent logos in the windows, and entered what might have passed for an old French bistro.

Inside: a long antique wooden bar, softly lit black and white striped banquettes, and a random array of old framed portraits on the walls—a reclining nude with fiery red hair, Charles DeGaulle, a smoking Keith Richards. The feel was dark and sexy, like a famous jazz bar or a carefully curated stage set. In fact, it was both. The restaurant had hosted many a funky quartet and had also been the stage set for *Sex in the City* and other shows.

Donna Finkelstein Nicholas was already seated at a banquette, an empty martini glass in front of her on the table.

It wasn't Vito's type of venue, and Donna Finkelstein wasn't his favorite type of client. As though she sensed Vito's unease with the surroundings, Donna began, "Raoul's is one of Michael's favorites. I think it's as close to a French type of restaurant as he could get Alex to eat at. Alex didn't like coming to Soho—he did it for Michael. He didn't like anything French either, except maybe French women. I think he was in love with that nude there on the wall. He had a thing for redheads, especially naked ones."

Vito was uncomfortable. He found Donna, with her short attention span, to be a difficult client to deal with, especially with the news he was about to deliver.

"I kind of like this place, maybe because Alex hated it. Are you sure you don't want a drink? You're the only frickin' private detective in the world that doesn't drink."

"No, thanks. I'll have a Coke."

"Fine," she said. "But you have to order the steak au poivre. That's what they're known for here."

Knowing he had already pushed his luck with the Coke, Vito knew he'd have to talk his way out of that too. But first, Donna would have to stop talking.

"So, what's so important that you couldn't tell me over the phone, or do you just enjoy having dinner with me, Vito?"

"Heh." He nodded at her wit. "Here's what I've got for you. I didn't find Alex, but I found his girlfriend. Her name is Heidi. She's German."

"German? That's a bit of a surprise. Somehow, I don't see Alex with a German girl. Swedish, Irish, Italian, Jewish—although most Jewish girls have brains, so that doesn't always work with him—but German? Germans are too strong, too like black and white, you know what I mean? I could even see him with an Asian, they're so obeying. But . . . German?"

Vito breathed deep and let her words fly by him. "Listen. There's more."

"More? You mean S&M or something? Maybe that was why he was with a German girl. But Alex was never good at taking orders—"

God help me, Vito said to himself. He had to interrupt her. "Stop. No, nothing like that. What I'm trying to tell you is something isn't right, and it has nothing to do with her nationality or kinks. I don't know how to say this, but . . . I don't think she's *real.*"

Donna laughed, her head swinging back with the broad movement that multiple martinis tend to cause. "Of course she's not real, Alex lives in a fantasy world. He's crazy."

"No, I mean something different here."

"Different?"

"Yes. Well, to start, it looks like she hangs out in a mannequin shop in Berlin."

"Alex with a mannequin." She started giggling. "That's what he needs, actually. It would be perfect, as long as he could—"

"No. Stop. There's more to this. I'm not kidding here. There was . . . a body, a dead man, a corpse, lying on the floor inside the shop where I met her."

"My God, that's strange even for one of Alex's girlfriends. It wasn't Alex, was it?"

"No. I don't know who the guy was, and I didn't stick around to find out."

"Well, did she murder this guy?"

Finally, Vito had hold of Donna's full attention. Time for a small lie.

"I don't know. I decided not to ask a lot of questions except as they pertained to Alex."

"So what did she say about Alex? Has she seen him?"

"She didn't say she'd seen him—but she said she had *spoken* to him just before I walked in."

Donna looked stunned. "Really? So Alex *is* alive."

Vito raised his finger. "Uh, not so fast."

"What? If the girl just spoke with him, then he's alive. I'm . . . surprised . . . although I guess I don't know why I should be. Well, did she say where he is?"

"Listen, Donna, when I said earlier that I don't think Heidi's real, I meant . . . I'm not sure she's *human*."

CHAPTER 36

For many, the unmeasurable time in a state somewhere between sleep and wakeful consciousness brings revelations of stark truths.

Solevetsky now saw Putin clearly: a man who idolized Stalin, who, by nature and training, was unable to share power, distrusting if not paranoid, and now threatened by dissidents and an increasingly restless population. He was a cornered animal.

The archbishop knew that his own growing unpopularity among the Russian people was the opportunity for Putin to eliminate a rival for his authoritarian rule.

Why hadn't Solevetsky seen it before? He had relied on his friend Putin, whose leadership and wars he had supported, to protect him, forgetting that Putin was a natural predator who dispensed deadly polonium to his rivals when he wasn't having them thrown out windows in foreign hotels.

Putin's curiosity—perhaps obsession—with artificial intelligence and Alex Nicholas was further proof that the man had gone mad with power. Did he really believe that there existed a creature of sorts created from artificial intelligence who could supplant or be an extension of the life of a human being, a real person? Only God could create man—and only God would promise immortality.

So this is what it had come to: a shepherd battling a wolf for the hearts and souls of the flock.

As he lay in his bed, Solevetsky realized that the Almighty Himself had entered his consciousness by way of this dream-like state in order to send him this warning. More than a warning, actually. A biblical command.

Solevetsky closed his eyes, the future resolving with great clarity: Putin, like Stalin before him, would shut down the churches, murder or exile the priests to Siberia, and consolidate his power over the people of Mother Russia.

The patriarch looked deep into his soul, searching for a sign, another vision of what was to come. With his eyes tightly shut he closed out the world around him, placing himself on a new spiritual plane, somewhere else, awake but reentering a dream-like world.

Suddenly soaked with a nervous sweat, he fully understood the meaning of his revelation.

Putin intends to murder me.

Thanks to this rare vision, a true gift from God, Solevetsky knew he had only one choice if he were to prevent his own murder and the destruction of the church. With God's help and, he was certain, approval, he would murder Vladimir Putin first.

CHAPTER 37

Paris

"My name is Sasha. I am a model."

"I can see that. Sasha . . . and what is your last name?" Michael asked for no reason except to make conversation while he tried to remember and figure out what had happened to him before he wound up in bed with this woman, and what, if anything had occurred between them while he . . . slept. And how to get her out of his room without insulting her or causing bigger problems.

"My last name? I am Sasha. That is all. That is how I am known."

"I see." He didn't. "One moment . . . okay?"

The woman shrugged and slid back under the blanket.

Unsure what to do, Michael opened his laptop, hopeful that, despite whatever the Russians had done to his computer, it still worked and that Alex was still there.

He was pleasantly surprised when the gold Greek Orthodox cross icon appeared on his desktop screen. He clicked on it and watched as the little circle revolved, taking longer than usual. They're probably watching everything I do on this now, he thought, as if they hadn't been doing it all along. He wondered if he'd been filmed in bed with Sasha. It would be a typical Russian move. Already, he'd decided not to ask her what, if anything, had gone on between them. He preferred not to know.

As he waited for Alex to appear, Michael's thoughts turned to the myriad of feelings he'd had for him during their lives together. On a disorderly timeline, his feelings for Alex traveled through deep brotherly love and respect and then passed through alternating and parallel feelings of frustration, disappointment, fear, resentment, anger, and confusion.

Growing frustrated over the never-ending spinning circle, he looked over at Sasha and realized that it was not Alex he needed to speak with. *What the hell am I doing?*

As Michael slowly recovered his equilibrium and returned to a more normal consciousness, he suddenly clicked off his computer and picked up his cell phone. He needed to call Samantha. It was three in the morning in North Carolina, but he could only imagine what she'd been going through during his disappearance,

Thank God his iPhone started up without a hitch. He dialed his wife and waited anxiously while it rang. As he did, he noticed something strange. He could swear he heard another phone ringing just outside his hotel door, in the hall. Seconds later, he heard three firm knocks on his door.

"Michael, are you in there? Open the door. It's Samantha."

CHAPTER 38

When she wasn't with Solevetsky, Anastasia lived in the massive building known as "the House on the Embankment" across the Moscow River from the Kremlin.

Built in the 1930s to house high-level Soviet officials, it was best known as the place of residence of the Soviet elite, many of whom were arrested and executed during Stalin's Great Purge. During this period, it had the highest rate of per-capita arrests and executions of any residential building in Moscow. Fully a third of its residents disappeared.

Now, ninety years later, the list of those who were murdered in Putin's own Great Purge included political opponents, human-rights activists, whistle-blowers, and reporters. Anastasia had known many of them.

The most prominent were Aleskei Navalany, poisoned then prosecuted, who died in prison after a short walk; Yevgeny

Prigozhin, aka "Putin's Chef," who died, along with his top associates, in a plane crash; Sergei Yushenkov, shot in front of his Moscow home; Anna Politkovskaya, shot dead in front of her apartment building; Aleksandr Litvinenko, poisoned with radioactive polonium-210 in London; Natalya Estemirova, shot dead near her home in Chechnya's capital, Grozny; Sergei Magnitsky, who died in pretrial detention after being tortured and denied medical care; Boris Nemtsov, shot dead gang-land style on a bridge near the Kremlin. And there were others, lesser-known figures.

Anastasia lived in fear that her lover would be Putin's next victim—and that she would be next in her building's long line of murdered residents, albeit purged by Stalin's self-proclaimed protégé.

Sitting on her faded brown couch, Anastasia anxiously answered her mobile phone.

It was the news she feared. Dmitri was to keep her abreast of any news related to Putin's quest for Alex Nicholas's special technology.

She congratulated her son on his team's discovery. "Your Putin must be quite pleased, no?"

"Yes, yes. He has just called her himself." Thanks to Bogolomov's expertise, all of his calls to her were encrypted and impervious to any of Bogolomov's fellow intel spies' electronic eavesdropping.

"Putin called the widow of Alex Nicholas? In America? He picked up the phone?"

"Well, *I* picked up the phone and set up the call, but, yes, he has spoken with her."

"That's most unusual. He must be . . . desperate . . . or he has lost his mind? I understand that you respect this man, but you know my feelings about him."

"I believe, knowing his KGB background, that he felt quite at ease questioning her for information. He was quite effective."

"Nevertheless, what exactly did she say?"

"The widow confirmed that the old computer is still in her home."

"Dmitri, tell me, when they capture this computer, will it give them what they need for Putin to be duplicated?"

There was silence. Then Dmitri spoke. "I believe it is possible, yes."

Anastasia tried to imagine the scene. "Didn't the widow think it was odd that our Russian president, the head of state, would call her?"

"The Americans are not the most well-versed on affairs outside their own country. She . . . ah . . . did not recognize the name Vladimir Putin."

"My God. Perhaps, Dmitri, she is fortunate to live in a place where such ignorance is possible. How soon will you have the computer?"

"Putin has already dispatched an agent, Dostoyevsky, to retrieve it. He is in New York as we speak."

She wondered whether Dmitri expected her to share all this information with Solevetsky or whether was he naïve to her agenda. Her son was aware of their affair and her loyalty to the archbishop—and of her disgust with Putin.

Perhaps by his silence, never openly acknowledging or questioning whether she would let Solevetsky know, was he satisfying himself that he had not betrayed Putin and the FSB?

It did not matter. Things were moving too fast. She needed to get to Solevetsky, make him aware of the additional computer—and tell him they had to speed up their plan.

CHAPTER 39

Paris

Michael opened the door and Samantha rushed into the suite's foyer, flinging her arms around him in a tight embrace. She was crying. "Oh my God, I can't believe I really found you. And at the Ritz, of course."

"How did you know I was here? I just woke up. I didn't even have a chance to call anyone."

"I got a message," she said breathlessly. "I don't know who it was from, but I followed the instructions. I was warned not to tell anyone or else, so I got on the next plane to Paris. I only told Karen and Sophia. What in the world *happened* to you?"

Michael proceeded to tell Samantha as much as he could remember, beginning with leaving his office an unknown number of days ago and entering a limo to JFK. After that, it was a series of fragmented mini-stories that possessed the coherence of dream logic: private jets, pseudo-doctors. "I think I was in Russia, Sam. And I'm pretty sure I met with—I know this is gonna sound crazy—Vladimir Putin."

"Putin? Seriously?"

Michael had never told her about Alex's suspicions that the Russians were after him, making his pronouncement even more implausible than it would have been, if that was possible. Samantha certainly had never seen Michael like this before, so dazed and confused.

She pointed at a chair in the foyer. "Sit down, honey. Are you okay? Do you even know how you got into the hotel?"

"I . . . don't know. I think I'm still on some sort of drug. Of course, it all had to do with Alex."

"Okay, don't worry. I'll get you help. I'll have the hotel call a doctor. My suitcases are downstairs, I'll have the bellman send them up."

Michael looked around, suddenly missing his phone and laptop. "I need to get to Alex and—"

He stopped and stood quickly, seeing that Samantha's attention had moved elsewhere. Her eyes shifted through the foyer entrance and into the room beyond. She took a quick step back, her eyes wide.

It was only then that Michael remembered.

He followed his wife, who was striding into the main room, where Sasha had just walked out of the bathroom. Except for the towel wrapping her hair, she was naked.

CHAPTER 40

Tonight, Andrei Popov would be in the presence of the one man he was certain was the closest to God. A devout follower of the Russian Orthodox Church, he would be serving dinner to His Holiness, Patriarch Solevetsky, tonight.

He looked forward to this evening. After working in the Kremlin for several years he had become accustomed to seeing and serving Vladimir Putin. But he had yet to meet the patriarch.

His mother and father would be proud of him, and he couldn't wait to tell them. They had been uncharacteristically insistent that he join them and Aunt Anastasia for dinner this evening. It was only when his superiors at the Kremlin demanded that he serve there instead that he had to turn his parents down. Now he knew why.

Putin had always been respectful in their very brief interactions, often offering an acknowledging glance or, on a rare festive occasion, even a smile. Popov had no dislike for the president and perhaps even admired him. After all, he had restored Russians' self-esteem and reestablished their position of power in the world.

But Popov did not care for how Putin appeared to conduct his personal life, divorcing and disrespecting his wife of many years and turning to much younger, flashier women. It went against everything he had been taught was right, moral, and ethical. Things he had been taught at home, by his parents and by the teachings of the Church. It was a troubling dichotomy in Putin's personality, leaving Popov with a deep ambivalence about his feelings for his leader, one that he struggled to reconcile.

When he allowed his feelings to go there, Popov was deeply suspicious of Vladimir Putin.

As he passed from the Kremlin's kitchen and into the anteroom outside the conference room, Popov appreciated the consistency and order of the two silver trays on the serving table in front of him, each with identical etched-crystal shot glasses of vodka, a folded red silk napkin placed in identical positions atop a white linen cloth and identical silver plates with equal—and generous—portions of caviar. On the patriarch's tray was a place card with his name elegantly engraved on it. This was unusual, as he was the only guest this evening.

But something else was unusual tonight: the presence of a man he had never seen before who appeared to scrutinize Popov as soon as he entered the room. Dressed in a gray suit, white shirt, and black too-thin tie, he didn't appear to work in the kitchen or on the staff. He was powerfully built and had all the earmarks of a former KGB type, likely now with the FSB. Why, Popov wondered, was he here, tonight? And who had sent for him?

CHAPTER 41

At times, Alex Nicholas admired his younger brother. At times, he resented him.

Michael had always been the good kid, the one who finished college, although he seemed to treat it like a six-year-long luxury cruise at his parents' expense. Alex was always the bad boy, Michael the boy scout. In their marriages, Alex was a self-proclaimed serial cheater; Michael was loyal. Alex ran an illegal gambling operation, his home and offices raided every few years by the NYPD; Michael was a corporate CEO.

Alex was delighted when Putin deposited Michael into bed at the Ritz with a Russian model and arranged for Samantha to find them. There was a poetic justice to the gesture, indicating to Alex a sense of humor or, perhaps, a deeper understanding by Putin of Alex's sentiments toward his brother. Either way, it was a welcome surprise.

But Alex would not let the gesture cloud his assessment of Putin, who he knew was an imminent threat to his life and Michael's.

As long as Putin needed them, he would tolerate their existence. Once he succeeded in duplicating himself in the cloud like Alex, they would be in mortal, or, as it were, immortal danger.

Sizing up their mutual enemy had become a nearly full-time job for Alex. His research had gone deep. As a result of closely monitoring the continued hacking of his software by Bogolomov, Alex had become aware of the activities of Bogolomov's mother, Anastasia. This connection led him to the patriarch's yacht, his residence in Saint Petersburg, Anastasia's apartment in the House on the Embankment, numerous security surveillance cameras and microphones, and both of their cell phones.

Now Alex knew that Solevetsky was being a very naughty patriarch. Putin and Solevetsky had each other to worry about. That was something.

But Solevetsky's desire to beat Putin to Alex's technology meant that the patriarch, like Putin himself, formed a dire threat to Alex and his brother.

In addition, defending against Bogolomov's assaults on his software had weakened Alex; he could feel his strength waning, his power fading more often than it had before the Russian hacks. He felt like he was expending more and more energy simply staying alive, so to speak. Never mind all the frantic research he'd been doing. And then there was Heidi . . .

Soon, Alex feared, he would need much more computer power, more powerful servers. Ironically, he was unsure how to acquire them.

In the meantime, he would fight back. He would fight them all.

CHAPTER 42

It was never openly spoken of, but it was well known among certain elements of the Kremlin staff: people died inside these walls. A seemingly healthy guest would be carried out on a stretcher—or a gurney—and then reported to be dead on arrival at the hospital. Often, the gurney arrived before the victim's first symptom.

The man in the gray suit, looking like an FSB thug, had unnerved Popov, even more so as he recalled the unusual series of questions regarding tonight's dinner from the woman he knew as Aunt Anastasia, a close friend of his parents. She often spoke with them about the patriarch, and he had overheard his parents speaking about Aunt Anastasia's special relationship with the priest.

Tonight, his instructions were clear: "Bring the tray into the conference room and serve the president and the patriarch." Not a word was to be spoken unless he was specifically addressed by President Putin or the guest, a highly unlikely occurrence.

Popov could feel it. Something was suspicious. On a recent visit to his parents' house, Aunt Anastasia seemed to be already aware of the planned dinner and peppered him with questions about the arrangements. Then it so happened that his parents urged him not to work this evening.

Suspicious.

His apprehension was consuming him. Was the patriarch in danger? Or perhaps Putin?

He looked at the trays and the glasses and the two cards and then made eye contact with the man who had been closely watching him. The man nodded almost imperceptibly, signaling it was time to take the trays to the conference room.

Popov picked up the two trays and proceeded toward the doors to the conference room. But just as he did, his rapid movement and a breeze of air caused by another server entering from a side door caused the name cards to slip off the trays. He turned, fearful of the FSB man's reaction, but noticed that the man's attention had already shifted to the newly arrived server.

He quickly placed the trays on a serving table and picked up the cards.

But just as he was about to replace the cards on the tray, he felt the presence of the man behind him. "What is the delay, Popov? Get in there."

Panicked, he quickly placed a card on each tray and entered the conference room. As he walked in, he was surprised by what he saw on the table: a gold chalice, a matching gold plate holding a small piece of bread, and a long gold spoon.

Was Putin going to receive Holy Communion here, tonight, from the patriarch himself? Surely no harm would come to a man receiving Communion. Nor could harm come to the man administering it on behalf of God. He felt relieved.

This was the twenty-second century. Russian presidents did not murder their patriarchs, and patriarchs did not murder Russian presidents, especially after Holy Communion.

He proceeded first to Putin, placing the tray with the glass of vodka, the caviar, and the engraved card with his name on it next to him on the table. Putin did not look up at him.

He moved toward the patriarch. Their eyes locked, then broke away quickly as he placed the other tray in front of him on the table.

As he turned around to leave the room, he could feel the eyes of both men boring through him. He exited through the doors and returned to the anteroom.

It was then that Andrei Popov realized that in his panic at hearing the man in the gray suit shout at him, he was not sure whether he had placed the proper name card on the appropriate tray.

CHAPTER 43

D onna Nicholas lived in the traditional colonial-style house on the quiet tree-lined street in Queens where her *allegedly*—a word she now used daily—dead husband, Alex Nicholas, had lived for years, even before they were married. The same one the cops one night had blocked off from both sides with a total of seven police cars and some twenty cops and then raided their home. All for a guy who'd never carried a weapon in his life.

Everyone believed Alex lived so well because his general insurance brokerage business, the Nicholas Agency, was successful, but it had only been a front to legitimize at least some of Alex's illegal profits from his gambling enterprise.

In her mid-forties, Donna still had the raw sexual appeal that had so attracted Alex. She loved Alex and hated him, both during their stormy marriage and in the three years since his death, of which—despite burials and even an urn of ashes delivered to her by the Greek Orthodox priest—she remained unconvinced. It was as though Alex had tried too much to be dead.

He had left her financially secure: a fully paid-for house, two million in cash he had hidden in the floorboards of their dining room, a million-dollar life insurance payout and a continuing share of the illegal but highly lucrative loan-sharking and bookmaking business that Michael was now running—or at least that was what everyone was trying to convince her was happening. She questioned how Michael, a straight-arrow businessman who'd never even bet on a horse or a sports team in his life, could run Alex's business, even with the assistance of Fat and Skinny Lester, who had worked for Alex for years. And all this while Michael continued to serve, at least during the day, in his role as CEO of a major legitimate financial services company, Gibraltar Financial.

It didn't make sense to Donna. It just wasn't possible.

Most recently her world was rocked by Vito Colucci, her hired PI, who returned with more questions than answers but some serious leads on Alex, including his discovery of Heidi. Lying in her bed, alone, naked, Donna was depressed over the thought of Alex having found a new life with a robot chick.

But for tonight at least, she would leave her anger at Alex aside. She would move on and satisfy the needs and longings that Alex could no longer fulfill.

With her laptop on her lap, she signed into iJewishMingle and, as she waited for her messages to pop up, reached for the half-empty bottle of wine on her night table and refilled her glass.

As Donna let the tart red wine touch her taste buds and course through her chest, relaxing her nerves while raising her anticipation, she was delighted to see that she had a new response to her profile: *Let's talk or meet!* It was signed *Alan from Rego Park*. His picture matched his written profile description—tall, well-built yet stocky, muscular, late forties, dark hair—although he didn't look like an Alan, whatever an Alan was supposed to look like.

Just what she needed, a Jewish guy from Queens. But what did she expect on this site? A gentile from Nebraska? And maybe after being married for several years to a nonpracticing, disbelieving Greek Orthodox from Queens who ran around on her, a Jewish guy from Queens might not be so bad. Little did he know she had been Donna Finkelstein before she became Donna Nicholas and, now on the dating site, *Donna Dees*.

She messaged him back, *Yes, let's start by messaging here.*

Alan: *Okay, it is nice to meet you. I enjoyed reading your profile.*

Donna: *What part of it did you like?*

Alan: *The photographs.*

She was hooked.

CHAPTER 44

Solevetsky dipped a silver spoon into the chalice of wine. "Jesus said unto his disciples, 'This is my blood of the covenant, which is poured out for many. Eat my flesh and drink my blood.'" He held out the chalice for Putin to sip the Communion wine, which he did without hesitation. Their eyes met again and Solevetsky, satisfied that the world would soon change, returned to his chair.

Solevetsky wondered how long it would take for Putin to feel the effects. The amount of wine sipped was minimal, but it would be sufficient to bring the dictator down quickly.

Putin reached over to his tray and brought the glass of vodka up to his eye level as he proposed a toast. "To Mother Russia."

"To Mother Russia—and to our Lord, Jesus Christ," Solevetsky responded.

They both downed their vodka.

Putin immediately poured another vodka in his glass, raised it, faced Solevetsky and said, "To loyalty and friendship. To *our* friendship."

Solevetsky returned the gesture, welcoming the warm glow from the second round of spirits.

Putin sat back, seemingly relaxed, and began serving himself caviar. "How do you like it? This one is my favorite, royal white sturgeon. In the 1700s, our exports of caviar financed the entire Russian navy. It was more valuable than oil." He pointed to his dish. "It glistens. It's almost as if the little eggs burst in your mouth."

They each dipped into their caviar again. They sat in silence, Putin seemingly absorbed in his own thoughts.

Finally, he looked up and broke the silence. "Do you really believe there is this God, this all-powerful being or spirit who created the world and to whom we will be introduced someday when we . . . " Putin hesitated and then made a sudden sharp gesture with his right hand toward his stomach. Solevetsky also noticed a slight flinch.

"Is everything all right?" Solevetsky asked, careful not to seem overly concerned or solicitous.

"Yes, yes, of course. You know, Boris, I don't indulge like this every day. My diet is normally a simple one. Nevertheless, back to my question—how sure are you about God, the afterlife, all of it?"

"I have no doubt whatsoever. But you know that already."

Putin reached again for his stomach, this time allowing his hand to rest there, however briefly. "Perhaps it was the

Communion that does not agree with me?" he said jokingly. "I know it's not the vodka."

If only he knew, thought Solevetsky. *He will, very soon.*

"Let us do another," Putin said, lifting his glass and pouring another vodka. Solevetsky did the same, this time feeling the warm liquid go down even more smoothly.

"As to your faith, Boris, I wish I had the same certainty. It would make facing death so much easier . . . almost satisfying."

"There is still time," Solevetsky said.

"Time for what?" Putin said weakly.

But before Solevetsky could answer, Putin pushed back his chair, his legs splayed wildly, his mouth open as he appeared to gasp for air or simply lose control of it.

Putin gripped the arm of his chair so hard that his knuckles looked like they would burst out of the skin. Half out of his chair, Putin gripped his stomach with his free hand. He reached for a button under the table, missing it twice with his finger until he finally pressed it.

Yet no one came.

He looked at Solevetsky. "What is happening?"

His hand gripped the side of the conference table. His breathing was heavy, his eyes opened and closed, his jaw dropped. In a desperate lunge he pulled himself back to the table, laid his head on it, and then raised it with obvious effort. "Help me . . . Father."

Solevetsky watched stoically at first, saying nothing. Putin begin to spit up, a saliva-like liquid streaming from his mouth as his head landed once again on the table, this time with a harsh finality.

"It is at your most powerful moment that the devil has found you," Solevetsky said.

Putin, seemingly confused, weakly raised his head and looked at Solevetsky. "What are you saying?"

"Vladimir Putin, do you ask God for forgiveness from your earthly sins? For your plots against the Church, against the Lord, against . . . your patriarch?"

"What have you done, Boris?" Putin said, raising his head to speak. He pressed the button again and again. No one entered the room.

"I have done God's work. Your Communion, it was poisoned."

Putin's head fell back onto the table, one arm falling off to the side. His body appeared still, lifeless, his eyes vacant, open unnaturally wide, as though he had seen the afterlife.

Solevetsky rose from his chair and took a last look at Putin's body. "May God have mercy upon your soul and may the angels rescue you from the abyss."

Feeling faint himself from the ordeal, he went to the conference room door, opened it and announced to the waiting staff and security men, "Your Putin is dead."

His work finished, Solevetsky needed to get to his car, which was waiting for him outside the building. It was time to get out of the Kremlin.

CHAPTER 45

MOSCOW

As Solevetsky approached the grand marble circular stairway, two of Putin's security detail caught up with him. "Your Holiness, please come with me. We must return to the room . . . You must administer the last rites."

Turning toward the guard, Solevetsky said, "It is too late. Last rites are for the dying, not the dead."

But the men moved to block the patriarch's path, and one pointed him back toward the hallway he had just traversed. "You must say a prayer . . . for the departed. It is necessary. Please follow us."

In the hallway, as they retraced their steps to the conference room, they passed by a hysterical Andrei Popov being dragged away by two men. As they approached him going the other way, Popov cried out, "Your Holiness, help me, please. I had no idea . . . " His face contorted, he tried to move in the direction of the patriarch but was firmly restrained and lifted off his feet. "Your Holiness," he continued, "please, please forgive me . . . please . . . help me. I did not know . . . I am innocent."

But Solovetsky and the guards paid no attention to his pleas as they approached the conference room where Putin's body lay. Popov's cries could be heard echoing through the Kremlin's marble-floored great hall as he disappeared.

The large heavy double doors had been closed since Solevetsky left moments earlier. The guards paused in front of the door. Solevetsky looked at the two men on either side of him, turning his head from one to the other. "He is in God's hands now."

Ignoring his words, they motioned him toward the door.

The two men each gripped a door handle and opened them simultaneously as though the patriarch were about to make a grand entrance. They moved to each side of the open doors, allowing Solevetsky to step into the room.

His mind had programmed itself to see what he expected, the scene as he left it, with Putin sprawled on the red carpeted floor, his mouth open, his eyes with the unmistakable vacant stare of the dead.

As he entered, his eyes traveled down to the carpet.

Expecting to see once again the bottom of Putin's leather soles, barely scuffed, he saw nothing but a broad expanse of plush red carpeting. Had they already moved the body?

He looked up, but as his eyes moved beyond the spot where Putin's body had been, he saw once again the immaculate black spit-shined shoes.

But the shoes—and the feet and rest of the fit body inside them—were standing upright.

CHAPTER 46

Since she was naked, Donna needed to remind herself that she was not on FaceTime or any other such visual app before she got up from her bed, which she hated to do, ever, but particularly late at night after a lot of wine. Alan had hooked her on iJewishMingle, but she wasn't quite ready yet to show off her most valuable assets.

Donna: *Excuse me for one minute. I have to do something.*

Donna: *Okay, I'm back. I needed more wine.*

Alan: *So, is Dees your real last name?*

Donna: *It's a bit early in our* relationship *to ask my real last name, isn't it?*

Alan: *No, especially since you've acknowledged that we have a relationship.*

Donna: *Well, my real name is Donna DOUBLE Dees.*

Alan: *You're not serious. If so, I love you already. We must meet.*

Donna: *I don't meet with men I see online.*

Alan: *Seriously? You're kidding. Then what are you doing here?*

Donna: *Toying with you, darling. BTW what is your last name?*

Alan: *Rubin, my name is Alan Ruben.*

Donna: *So which is it—Ruben or Rubin?*

Alan: *Oh, I see, that was a typo. It's Rubin.*

Alan: *So, I assume you are divorced, or are you still married and simply playing around?*

Donna: *I happen to be a widow. Before that I was married. And divorced, twice. And then I married again and now I am a widow.*

Alan: *Oh, I'm sorry. How long ago did your husband pass away?*

Donna: *Three years ago. I think.*

Alan: *You think?*

Donna: *If you knew my husband—Alex—you'd understand.*

Alan: *I'm sorry, but I guess I don't understand. What do you mean? Perhaps I'm being too forward?*

Donna: *No, it's just he was into a lot of things, gambling, things like that. He was also screwing around with any woman under 40 that moved, under thirty even if they didn't move. He's a guy that should have never married but couldn't stand to be alone. Yet he couldn't live with any woman who made any demands on him—and by demands, I mean something as simple as going to a friend's wedding while a big game was on or not leaving his girlfriend's black lace panties in the car. He was selfish.*

Alan: *He sounds like a not very nice person.*

Donna: *Actually, he was a great guy, just not a great husband. He was generous, kind, a lot of fun but a handful. And a son of a bitch.*

Alan: *Did YOU make a lot of demands?*

Donna: *Why would you suggest that?*

Alan: *I don't know. Just a suspicion, I guess.*

Donna: *A good one, actually. You must be very intuitive.*

Alan: *I am. So did you make a lot of demands?*

Donna: *No shit. I'm high maintenance. But so was he, believe me. He was so high maintenance he needed a fulltime mechanic for a wife.*

Alan: *So the two of you must have made a charming couple.*

Donna: *We did, at times, about fifteen minutes each day. The rest of the time was a nightmare. But Alex was generous, we lived well. I mean he hated fancy restaurants unless they served steak or lobster. He left me well off and he was very protective, as long as he didn't have to protect you when a big game was on tv. Then Jack the Ripper could come and get you and he wouldn't get up from his chair. So, tell me, are you like that?*

Alan: *No, not at all. I don't watch television.*

CHAPTER 47

Vladimir Putin stood straight, erect, with perfect posture, facing Solevetsky not more than four feet away. Stunned, Solevetsky was speechless. He ran through multiple possible scenarios, trying to understand what had occurred, a miracle from God not included among them.

No, he had been discovered, exposed, duped. "God has answered my prayers," he finally said, weakly, hoping against all reason that the truth of what he'd done was not known. Feeling dizzy, he felt his skin burning and he struggled to remain standing, sure that the pressure of the situation was taking its toll on him physically. He didn't know what to do with any part of his body. It was as though he were imploding all over, simultaneously.

He felt an urge to touch his skin, anywhere, just to alleviate the itch, the burn, the pain. Suddenly, the weight of his notorious gold watch was more than his left wrist and arm could bear. At that moment, nothing was more critical to him than to remove that watch from his burning wrist. Pushing back the cuffs of his sleeve, he reached for it with his right hand, his fingers searching for the steel clasp on the underside. But as he rolled the watch over on his wrist to access the clasp, he was unable to perform the task.

Remaining still, Putin spoke calmly. "I'm afraid that your God has answered *my* prayers. You have overestimated your own influence and that of your Church. Did you seriously believe that you—"

But Solevetsky's body had caught up with him, no longer able to stand. He threw himself into the nearby chair, the one Putin had sat on during their caviar-and-vodka meeting. He felt a wrenching pain throughout his stomach as though it were hemorrhaging deep inside him. And then he saw his blood, gushing from his mouth, splattering onto the white silk tablecloth.

Through fading light, he watched Putin observing him like something in a test tube. He felt like he had been squeezed inside that tube. Unsure what to do with his arms, he clutched his chest, which was on fire inside, as though acid were running through it. He gasped for breath, but his lungs too were on fire.

Despite his torment, his mind understood the irony of his situation. He had been poisoned by the man he thought he had poisoned.

Like an observer in a zoo, Putin watched him, turned away, drank the remaining vodka in his glass and placed the glass back on the table.

"The FSB wishes you a safe journey," he said as he left the room.

The security men moved toward Solevetsky. There was only darkness. He remembered, too late, that he had forgotten to pray.

CHAPTER 48

D onna couldn't sleep. With a half empty bottle of wine remaining by her bedside, she refilled her glass. Propped up on two pillows, she inhaled another glass of the smoky chardonnay. She put her head back on the pillow, and her eyes scanned the space above her until they zeroed in on a tiny object on the ceiling. She believed it to be an insect of some sort. Before, Alex would kill them and then throw them into the toilet.

Because of the nature of his business and the people he did business with, Alex had installed all sorts of nearly invisible surveillance cameras around the house, different types of bugs. But this "bug" was right over the bed. Had she never noticed it before? It would be just like Alex to film them having sex. Or was it just an insect?

Alex always knew the difference between the tiny black cameras and a real bug. It was one of the few things he was good for.

But, again, the question was, how long had it been there? And if it was a tiny camera, and assuming it was Alex who was behind its installation, *from where* was he watching? It wasn't moving—it was one of his cameras.

She thought about what had gone on in the house since Alex's murder, since he had gone. She had taken only a few men to her bed, local Queens guys who had wanted to have sex with her for years. He must have watched. He had always been a voyeur.

She still felt his presence in the rooms as she went by, particularly the ones he'd lived in all day, his ball room with all the sports memorabilia—an autographed set of Muhammed Ali's red boxing gloves in a Plexiglas display box and baseball bats signed by Mickey Mantle, Hank Aaron and Dave Winfield, all in a glass case hanging on the wall.

And then there was Alex's computer, an old Apple desktop lying on the floor hidden behind his desk chair. He had stopped using it and had switched to a new laptop, which was long gone. Michael had supposedly borrowed it right after Alex's funeral, but he never returned it, leaving Donna to wonder, as she did about so many things.

She felt his presence throughout the house, his scent, the smell of his Aqua Velva, perhaps still on a towel she hadn't used . . . since. She swore she could even smell the stale scent of the Lucky Strike cigarettes he stopped smoking years before.

But it was more than that. She felt not only his past, his remnants, but also his present, maybe even his future; she felt his spirit, all around her, like a letter from an eternity she didn't even believe in, challenging her skepticism over her faith and her vacillating grief.

Was Alex dead? Probably. Deep down she did believe he was gone . . . but then she didn't or . . . then she did. Maybe the uncertainty was just enough to keep her from feeling totally alone, leaving her just enough hope for her to feel safe, because underneath her bitchy persona, just like Alex, she was too insecure to be by herself, especially when it was dark outside.

On the other hand, maybe it was time to find another lover, someone she was sure was alive, someone to watch over her, and not through a camera. She drank the remaining wine in the bottle, picked up her laptop, signed in to *iJewishMingle*, and clicked on the name "Alan R."

Alan: *Good evening, Mrs. Dees.*

Donna: *I've been thinking, perhaps we should meet.*

CHAPTER 49

Moscow

As she entered her apartment in the House on the Embankment, Anastasia waited anxiously for word from Solevetsky of Putin's death.

Gripping her mobile phone in one hand, she turned the key, pushed opened the door and switched on the lamp on the antique console table near the door.

The evening lights of Moscow and the glittering Kremlin reflected through the small opening in the curtains draped across the tall windows in the living room, illuminating the shelves of antique books lining the walls: the prized collection of the patriarch.

But Anastasia sensed that something was wrong. No one had been in the apartment since she had left earlier in the evening to go out to dinner just down the street with her friends. Yet, as she surveyed the room . . . it was those living room drapes. She had left them slightly opened, but she was sure they were open wider now. She moved to the window.

She swept the curtains aside, opening them as wide as they would go. Looking out, she could see the nearby cafés and bars and an assortment of Moscow nightlife. She picked out the café where she had just dined. Had someone entered the apartment and watched for her return?

Had the FSB planted a surveillance device? Or was someone still there, inside, watching her? Waiting.

She moved through the apartment, turning on each light she passed, checking the closets, under the beds, behind the curtains, inside the oven, the refrigerator, her heart racing as she inspected each place.

She wanted to call Solevetsky but did not want to disrupt him or bring any attention to herself at such a critical time. She would hear from him soon enough.

Instead, she pressed the number for her son and put the cell phone to her ear. She knew that she could always rely on Dmitri to protect her or alleviate her fears. He answered immediately.

"Dmitri—"

But he interrupted her. "Mother, the patriarch is dead. I wanted to tell you in person, but I fear . . . " He did not continue. His words hung in the air.

She stopped, momentarily unable to process what she'd heard.

"This is impossible," she said but stopped again before continuing. If Dmitri was correct and the worst had occurred, their phones could be tapped. They would be listening. She had to be cautious. She understood that Dmitri too was unable to verbalize all his thoughts. But she had to know more.

"What has happened?"

"He was poisoned, by the caviar. The server . . . Popov, they said did it. He is dead too."

"No—"

"They are blaming him."

"And Putin," she said, "he is . . . " Another unfinished sentence, dangling fragments. She wondered whether her son knew how to fill in the omitted words. Did he—or Putin—know of Solevetsky's plan to poison Putin through his Communion? And, either way, what had happened? What had gone wrong?

Dmitri never finished the sentence. At least not that Anastasia could hear. Despite the risk, she had to tell him. "He is mad, your Putin," she said into the phone. "He will destroy Russia, maybe much more. You must stop him."

She heard his voice through the static but could not make out his words. Her mind was racing. Were they coming for her next? There was one more message, a terrible secret she had withheld from him since the beginning that she had to tell him, now, before it was too late. He would be upset.

"Dmitri, your father . . . " But the ominous silence at the other end caused her to check the phone's screen before she continued. As she feared, the connection had been lost.

She redialed his number. After several seconds of silence, she pulled the phone from her ear and looked at the screen— "No Service."

She walked to the kitchen and picked up the landline that she hadn't touched in months. She had to reach him. There was no dial tone. She tried her cell phone again; its screen was black.

Panicking, her legs weakening, she moved quickly to the front door. Thoughts of the history of the building—more deaths and its disappearances per capita, residents being dragged out of the building and shot on the sidewalk—raced through her mind.

She reached the door and turned the handle and, although it turned, the lock would not disengage. She pulled on the door—it was immovable. She raced back to the living room; she would open the windows and scream for help. She pulled up on the lower pane, but it wouldn't move. It appeared to have been sealed. It had to have been done recently. She remembered opening it slightly just yesterday. She tried the others, with the same result.

She looked out the window, down to the street, eight stories below. A single police car and an ambulance sat in front of the building's entrance.

She turned back to the room and her eyes caught what had probably troubled her all along. It was in the antique leather-bound book spines, in fading shades of blue, deep red and green, framed with gold lines, the patriarch's books. They covered the entire length of one wall and part of another. But it was one shelf, actually a third of the shelf, that caught her eye.

Now, looking at them from the other end of the room, she saw that ten or so of the books were sticking out slightly more than the others, a couple of centimeters out of place. Solevetsky himself, when he visited, was the only one to ever handle them, and he was meticulous about their placement.

She went into the kitchen and returned with a small step-ladder, placed it under the offending shelf, stepped up, and tried with one hand to push the books back into alignment with the others. They wouldn't move.

She raised herself up another step and pulled out two of the volumes, standing them up nearby on the shelf. Stretching to reach, she did the same with three more, opening up the space that had been behind them. There was something there.

She pulled two more books off the shelf and held them in her hand. She raised herself up another step to get a closer look at what had been hidden behind the books. When she saw what it was, she dropped the books to the floor.

Frozen, she stared at the clear plastic sandwich-type bag of white powder, like flour or sugar. But the two devices attached to the bag told a different story. One was an unmarked steel box the size of a pack of cigarettes. The other was a digital clock, with numbers counting down.

After several seconds, she understood that the numbers most likely represented how many seconds she had to live. 17, 16, 15, 14, 13, 12, 11, 10, 9 . . .

CHAPTER 50

Paris

Michael still had work to do in Paris, and some explaining to do. Preferring a more discreet, under-the-radar hotel, he and Samantha had checked out of the Ritz and into the Hotel D'Aubasson, a comfortable boutique hotel in the 6th arrondissement, where they had stayed once before.

"Samantha, first, I have no idea how I wound up in that room at the Ritz. Obviously, I'd been drugged by Putin's people."

"That I can understand, strange as it may seem. But—"

"I know, how did Sasha wind up in my room?"

"Correction," Samantha said, "how did Sasha wind up *in your bed*? And, even better, did you two have sex?"

"I swear, I have no idea whether we had sex. I certainly don't remember doing anything with her. All I remember is one day I was in Moscow, and that's pretty foggy in itself, and then I woke up at the Ritz in bed with her."

"Didn't you ask her if you'd had sex?"

"The thought crossed my mind, but . . . no, I didn't. The best I can figure is that placing me in that bed with her was some sick joke either by Putin or, maybe more likely, Alex."

"The stuff dreams are made of," Samantha said in her finest sarcastic manner.

Later, while Michael was enjoying a breakfast croissant and coffee and scanning the *New York Times International Edition*, two articles caught his attention. The first was on the front page:

Russian Orthodox Patriarch Is Dead - Poisoned by Kremlin Server Who Committed Suicide

TASS, the official Russian state news agency, reported this morning that the head of the Russian Orthodox Church, His Holiness Patriarch Boris Solevetsky, has died, a result of a poison allegedly placed in his caviar by a server while he was dining inside the Kremlin. Kremlin security personnel immediately apprehended the server, Andrei Popov, but not before he swallowed the same poison-laced caviar reportedly used to kill the patriarch. Popov's death was ruled a suicide. He was pronounced dead on the scene.

The second article was in the arts section, announcing an exhibit at the Musee D'Orsay with an invitation from the museum to speak with a famous French artist who had been dead for over 130 years.

An unexpected call interrupted his serenity.

From the day his brother married her, Donna Finkelstein Nicholas drove Michael crazy. "She's got the attention span of a flea," he'd often told his brother.

So when he saw her name pop up on his cell phone, he prepared for his blood pressure to rise.

"Alex is spying on me," she said before Michael could even say hello.

"What are you talking about?"

"There's a bug which I think is a camera right above my bed. I think your brother has been watching me have sex."

"Come on, Donna. I find that hard to believe." Although he had to admit, not much harder to believe than arranging for Michael to wake up next to a Russian model.

"And it's none of his business who I'm screwing."

"Nor is it any of mine," Michael said, hoping the call was near its end.

"And that's not all," she said, dashing his hopes. "I hired a private eye, Mr. Vito Colucci, to look for your brother,"

"Do you seriously believe that a private detective is going to track down Alex? Has he tried Saint Michael's cemetery?"

"Not yet, but hold the presses—he found Alex's girlfriend. Or one of them, or his latest, whatever."

"Okay," Michael said, skeptical but curious. "Who is she?"

"Her name is Heidi, and she lives in Berlin. Just down the block from Hitler's bunker."

"A coincidence, I'm sure. Does she have a last name?"

"Well, this is where it gets strange."

CHAPTER 51

It was the first time Donna Nicholas had had sex except with herself in two months. She wasn't sure which she preferred.

As she lay in bed, she pulled the covers over her and waited, listening for the water to go off in the bathroom. She wondered whether Alan—she suspected his name wasn't really Alan—would be returning to the bed for more of her, returning to the bed to sleep, or coming out of the bathroom to dress and leave. She hoped it was the latter.

What was he doing in there for so long?

She heard the ping of a cell phone, not hers. Seeing the light from Alan's cell phone screen on the bureau at the other end of the bedroom, she got out of bed and went to it.

Twisting her head around the corner of the wall, she checked the bathroom door. It was still shut, so she picked up the phone and read the text, which had just arrived on Alan's phone: *Did you find the computer?*

She scrolled up, looking for more messages, but that was the only one.

She checked the bathroom door again, still closed, and the water was still running. She moved to it and placed her ear against it. There was no sound other than the running water. She knocked, gently. No response.

"Alan?" she whispered. She knocked again, this time more firmly. Still nothing. She turned the door handle and slowly began to open the bathroom door. "Alan?" she said again, not so softly. Still hearing nothing, she looked inside. The bathroom was empty.

She turned off the water, left the bathroom and looked out the into the hallway and to the top of the staircase. She saw the shadow, someone moving past a reflected light in the next room, the room that had been Alex's study, or ball room.

She called out again, louder this time. "Alan, where are you?" She heard a noise, some shuffling, coming from Alex's study. She looked in; the man had been using Alex's old computer. Dressed only in black briefs, he turned and faced her. His right fist was closed, hiding something.

She recalled that odd call from a while ago . . . the man asking about Alex's computer. She tried to remember his name. "What did you do? What's that in your hand?"

He just looked back at her, his face tightened as though he were angry. It was the same look she had seen when he had finished with her, earlier.

"And . . . who are you?"

As she approached him, he tried to avoid her and proceed into the bedroom. She grabbed his hand; he tightened his fist and tried to push her away. She held on tightly and bit into his hand as hard as she could. An object fell out of his hand and dropped to the floor.

He said something—it sounded to her like *suka*, which she assumed was a foreign curse word. She went to pick the object up off the floor, but he beat her to it, shoving her aside and hard into the wall. But not before she saw what it was: a computer flash drive.

He left her on the floor as he went into the bedroom to grab his clothes.

"Get the fuck out of here," she said sharply from the hallway.

She watched him as he finished dressing in the bedroom and, without making eye contact, passed her and went down the steps toward the front door. Suddenly she remembered the name of the caller.

"Are you Vladimir?" she called out.

That got his attention. He stopped at the door, turned, and looked up at her as she stood at the top of the stairs.

"They call me Dostoyevsky, but you'd be wise to forget you ever saw me."

CHAPTER 52

D mitri Bogolomov feared for his life.

He and his team had spent the last forty-eight hours analyzing the contents of the flash disk Dostoyevsky had uploaded to them. It was time to inform Putin of the results.

Grieving over his mother's death in the explosion at her apartment in the House of Embankment, he dreaded meeting face-to-face with the man he knew was responsible for her murder.

As he walked down the hallway toward Putin's office, he was also convinced now that Putin knew not only of his mother's hatred of him but also that she had been the now-deceased patriarch's lover. This would leave Bogolomov as a dead man in waiting.

Just before he arrived at the desk outside Putin's office, Bogolomov noticed a man in civilian dress, a navy-blue sport coat and red tie, leaving the suite of offices and heading toward him.

At first, he thought it was Putin, perhaps running an errand before returning for their meeting. They came face-to-face with each other, even making brief eye contact, before the man who appeared to be Putin turned down another corridor without showing Bogolomov any recognition. Only then did Bogolomov realize it was *not* Putin. The resemblance was stunning except for one minor detail: the presence, Bogolomov noted, of a small black mole on the man's left cheek, close to his ear.

As he entered Putin's office, it struck him that Putin wore a navy-blue sport coat and red tie, exactly as his body double had. It was smart and, in truth, not all that surprising. But Dmitri's mind now moved to more important concerns. Like whether he would leave this meeting alive.

Putin's face revealed no hint, far too practiced in deception to send a clear signal.

"Please accept my condolences on your mother's passing," Putin said as soon as Bogolomov sat down.

Passing? Bogolomov thought. But Putin did not wait for a response. "So, what news do you bring? I gather that Dostoyevsky has done his work."

"Yes, Mr. President. We have analyzed the contents of Alex Nicholas's old computer from the data supplied by Dostoyevsky."

"And?" Putin was impatient.

"I am pleased to report to you that we have the codes necessary to duplicate you onto the cloud."

"This is excellent, excellent. Good work. What is the next step then?"

"We need to download all the input you have provided over the past months—your history, your decisions, your tastes, etcetera—to establish your . . . persona. This will be done at the same time that we refine the technical programming."

Bogolomov did not want to point out that, at this point, most of the remaining work would be done by his technical staff and that Bogolomov's expertise was no longer required for the project to be completed.

"How long will this process take?"

"You should be . . . *live* . . . in a week, sir."

Putin rose from his chair, signaling the end of the meeting, and as he departed, Dmitri Bogolomov calculated that he had a week left to live.

CHAPTER 53

Paris

They had returned to their favorite bistro, Chez Dumonet, where they had dined on their Paris trips for more than twenty years. On the left bank's Rue du Cherche-Midi, it looked like a stage set for the century-old bistro that it was—warm dimmed lighting, white lace curtains, cut-glass room dividers, bentwood chairs, black and white tile floor, an old zinc and mahogany bar.

Samantha, now in her mid-forties, was a few years younger than Michael, slim, fit, stylishly attired in a short black dress, wearing a string of pearls, carrying a small black Hermes bag, and flashing a four-carat diamond ring from a famous jeweler in Florence on her slender, tanned finger, accenting her nails, which had been professionally lacquered in bright yellow for the summer. They had met in Manhattan right after college. She'd graduated from NYU and was an investigative reporter for a popular New York television network. Michael had earned his graduate degree at the New School for Social Research in Manhattan and was working, although quite bored, at the Chase Manhattan Bank on Wall Street. It was, and remained, a love affair.

Samantha still appeared noncommittal regarding Michael's earlier model-bedding explanation and, although he dared not verbalize it, he felt shortchanged. After all, if in fact he did have sex with Sasha and had to suffer Samantha's skeptical judgment, at least he should have been able to remember the experience.

Sensing her coolness toward him, he wanted to clear the air. "Samantha, I've just been kidnapped, hauled into Russia, drugged, interrogated, and then thrown on a plane and smuggled into, fortunately, Paris. It's a miracle I'm here at all. Don't we have other things to worry about?"

"We can worry about more than one thing at a time. It's a mark of a civilized person. I'll get over it. Even if you did have sex with her, it's not like *you* arranged it or, evidently, even remember it." Then pivoting, as though she'd heard enough, at least for now, she asked, "How's your beef bourguignon?"

Michael was relieved with the sudden change of subject. "As good as ever. A testament to Gallic genius." In a deep burgundy sauce and served over buttered noodles, Chez Dumonet's beef bourguignon was always a special occasion in itself for him. As he devoured it, he could feel Samantha's critical gaze over his dinner indulgence. As always, he knew she wished he had ordered the half portion.

"Did they get what they needed to . . . duplicate Putin?" Samantha asked. "That's what this was all about, wasn't it?"

"No, I don't believe they got what they needed."

"Well, then how were you able to go free? Why would Putin let you go? The Russians don't give up any prisoners or hostages without a fuss, without some sort of trade. You know, we get one or two innocent Americans back and they get, like, twenty of their spies in return."

"No, you're right." Michael looked around him and the lowered his voice. "Alex made a deal with Putin."

"What kind of a deal? What did Alex have to offer Putin? He wouldn't be crazy enough to give up the secrets behind his . . . existence, those source codes you've talked about? Would he?"

"No, I'm sure he didn't, because once he gives them up, it's possible he'd be vulnerable. The Russians might be able to alter or . . . delete him."

"So, what kind of information did Alex have that was worth anything to Putin?"

"Alex had uncovered a plot to murder Putin, a planned assassination by someone very close to him, and he traded that information for my release. Or at least Putin agreed to let me out of Moscow and put me on that jet to Paris."

"And how would you know this?" Samantha said with a skeptical look.

"Alex told me . . . and he said something else."

She waited for it.

"If Putin's people are able to duplicate him on a computer, like Alex, he'll surely murder us, Alex and me, and anyone else he believes could be a threat to his virtual existence."

DEATH IN THE KREMLIN

"Why would he now want to kill you, either of you?"

"He wants to be the only human in the digital world, the only one who is immortal."

"Okay, then I understand wanting to eliminate Alex, but why you?"

"I know too much, and my computer may still have enough information or clues to help someone else re-create Alex's software."

"Michael, we can't go on living like this, always under threat."

"I agree. But we have a plan."

"*We?*" Samantha said with that look of astonishment, skepticism, and condemnation that Michael had only seen when it concerned his relationship with Alex.

"Alex is helping," he said softly, "but my part of the plan came from a document I was reviewing at the office, at Gibraltar, just before I left for, as it turned out, Moscow. I didn't put it together until Alex and I began planning our move."

"What could anything in your corporate world have to do with this thing with Putin?"

"It's called a 'poison pill.' It's designed to discourage a hostile takeover of a company. In this case, it will be something quite different, of course, but the theory behind it still works. Trust me."

"God help us," Samantha said.

And whether it was by the intervention of the aforementioned deity, the maze of the internet traffic's invisible crossing wires, or the machinations of his dead and virtual brother, Michael received at that very moment a text from Dmitri Bogolomov.

CHAPTER 54

Paris

Like Alex Nicholas, Vincent van Gogh was surprisingly busy for a dead man.

Michael remembered the announcement in the *Times* about the famous French artist who had been dead for 130-plus years, and since he had some time to kill before meeting Bogolomov, he decided to walk over to the Musee D'Orsay to see the special exhibit, "Bonjour, Vincent."

He was familiar with the artist's work from his regular travels to Saint-Remy, where van Gogh spent a year in an asylum for the mentally ill, right after cutting off his ear and just before committing suicide by shooting himself in the chest. Michael often followed van Gogh's own walks in Saint-Remy, as they were marked by the small brass markers identifying his path through the town.

But the reason Michael wanted to see the exhibit was the headline in the paper inviting visitors to chat with a new artificial-intelligence version of Van Gogh himself, displayed for audiences on a digital screen.

From what Michael had read, it appeared that the process the scientists followed was, at least superficially, similar to what Alex's creators had performed. They had reviewed and dissected more than nine hundred of Van Gogh's letters, input multiple biographies and other published material, and set up algorithms to duplicate his persona.

Michael was unsure how the technology compared with what Alex's experts had created in their secret breakthrough, but he doubted it could be anywhere near as sophisticated. Alex was not an interactive museum display, after all. He was real.

═══

Michael approached the display. Van Gogh, in a period-typical blue suit and high-collared shirt, sat on a wooden stool beside one of his paintings. His hands rested casually on the upper part his trousered legs. His face, at least initially, was expressionless, but his red hair and close-cropped beard and piercing eyes portrayed an intensity consistent with the famous tortured artist.

Michael leaned into the microphone in front of the display screen. "Why did you commit suicide?" he asked. He had read that this was one of the most popular questions.

Van Gogh moved around in his chair, his face now animated. His hand went to his chin as though he were finally contemplating the question after a hundred and thirty-four years. He was amazingly lifelike, at least FaceTime or Zoom-like real.

He spoke in English with an English accent. "My dear visitor, my suicide is a heavy burden to bear. In my darkest moments, I believed that ending my life was the only escape from the torment that plagued my mind." van Gogh hesitated. "I saw no other way to find peace."

"Do you have any advice for someone who is similarly tormented?" Michael asked.

Van Gogh didn't move this time. "Yes—cling to life, for even in the bleakest of moments, there is always beauty and hope."

Michael decided to test him. "Do you know any other virtual human beings?"

Van Gogh's body stiffened, his head tilted slightly, his eyes narrowed. "There are others," he said.

This wasn't in the script, Michael thought. "Who are they?" he asked.

Van Gogh paused. He appeared momentarily frozen. Was he thinking? Was his system searching for the answers? Had Michael's question overloaded the software?

Finally, he answered. "I have spoken with Siri and Alexa."

"Anyone else?" Michael said.

"Beethoven is coming."

Michael had read that the same developers were working on bringing Beethoven to life next.

He said farewell to the painter's solemn simulacrum and turned to leave.

It was time to meet Bogolomov.

CHAPTER 55

Paris

Dmitri Bogolomov had agreed to meet with Michael but specified that it had to be at the location he chose, the Church of Saint-Sulpice, a Catholic church in in the Latin Quarter of the 6th arrondissement in Paris.

Michael was relieved, as he knew the location well, having once entered the cathedral as a tourist. The church became well-known as a location in the Dan Brown book and film of *The Da Vinci Code*. Michael wondered if Bogolomov was aware of that association.

As he approached the entrance, walking past the row of chestnut trees, he noticed a young man sitting on a bench, his face partially obscured by a newspaper. He was sure it was Bogolomov, scoping out the church, probably to be sure Michael came alone. The newspaper was the French daily *Le Monde*, but Michael observed that it was being held upside down. Bogolomov, Michael reasoned and hoped, was a computer techie, not a seasoned FSB agent.

Michael went up the several steps to the front doors and, without looking around him, slowly opened one of the heavy old wooden doors. The church was empty, lit only by some late afternoon sunlight coming through the stained-glass windows and a series of ivory-colored candles arrayed throughout the nave. Out of habit, he bowed slightly, crossed himself, and walked on the ancient stone floor toward the altar, stopping halfway before taking a seat at the far-right end of one of the rows.

In a few minutes, Michael heard the creaking sound of the doors. He turned and saw the young man whom he had observed on the bench outside cautiously enter the cathedral. They made eye contact, Michael nodded slightly, and Bogolomov advanced toward him and took a seat beside him. They spoke in a whisper, each of them facing forward toward the altar.

"Who are you?" Michael asked.

"I am Dmitri Bogolomov."

"Thank you. I just needed to ask," Michael whispered. "I must admit, in view of your position and all that has just occurred, I was surprised you would want to meet with me. Or even *could* meet."

Bogolomov nodded soberly. "Terrible things have occurred—and more will occur, soon. I was unsure who to turn to, especially considering these unique circumstances. Your brother offered me a lifeline; we have been communicating."

"You are sure this version of Alex is real, then?"

"I am the one who convinced my president that the virtual Alex Nicholas is real."

Michael let that sink in for a minute. "I see. And your own intelligence people believe this to be true?"

This appeared to take Bogolomov by surprise. "Why . . . yes . . . are *you* not sure yourself? He is *your* brother."

"I know. That's true. But there have always been . . . questions, suspicions, that this virtual version is some sort of manipulation on his part, a deception and that he might still be alive, somewhere."

"You must mean in Las Vegas. Living with the whores."

"Showgirls," Michael said defensively.

"Yes, of course."

"So, why, after my kidnapping and my experience in Moscow at the hands of your president do you want to meet with me?" Michael needed to verify what he hoped Alex had established with Bogolomov.

"You must understand, I am putting my life and that of my family in grave danger by doing this. Should I be discovered here with you, I will be dead or at least imprisoned."

"Why would you even return to Moscow?"

"I have no choice. My wife and family, the ones who are still alive anyway, are there. They would never be allowed to leave, certainly not now. I must return."

"I have to admit, I didn't expect to wake up in the Ritz with that young lady in the bed with me."

"He did that as an accommodation to your brother. I think Alex requested it that way. He has an unusual sense of humor, no?"

"Yes. That sounds like Alex. But why was I released at all?"

"We retrieved as much information as we could from your phone and computer. You were set free, however, only because your brother provided Putin with information about an attempted assassination plot. The information was valuable, to say the least. Although it had terrible consequences for me which I would prefer not to discuss here, now."

"I understand. This conforms to what Alex told me. He doesn't always share everything with me. Occasionally too, he is inaccurate, or his memory is faulty. He's often, let's say, *overloaded* with data. Not unlike when he was . . . alive."

"But more recent events have occurred," Bogolomov said. "One of our FSB operatives located an old computer of your brother's. The contents were uploaded to us. It gave us all the information and data necessary for us to duplicate Putin, just as was done for your brother."

"I see. That certainly changes things."

"I needed to warn you," Bogolomov said, "Putin is suffering from a deterioration of his senses. It has distorted his judgment. It is a very dangerous situation . . . for the world."

"But Putin is still in control of his senses, his facilities. He's alive, is he not?"

"Yes, yes, of course. However, he is ill, although he hides it. Nevertheless, once we duplicate him, he will live in *both* worlds, here as he is now, on earth as a human—and in the virtual world as a creature of AI, living in the cloud. Whenever he ultimately expires here, he will only be in the cloud, like your brother."

"Okay, I understand. But what exactly are you warning me of—just that Alex will soon have company in the cloud?"

"No, there is more, much more."

"Then what is it? What is happening?"

"Putin believes he's going to die . . . soon. He has employed a body double to go in his place to some events to preserve his energy—and to take a bullet or poison intended for the real Putin. I recently passed this man in the corridor outside Putin's office. The only way I knew it wasn't Putin was due to a small black mole on his left cheek. What I am saying is, Putin intends to leave behind an all-powerful Russia who has defeated her greatest enemy—plus a personal legacy placing him amongst our greatest czars and Stalin. It is all about this legacy, his place in history, and, of course, revenge and resentment."

"How will he do that?"

"Once we have empowered him with the same capabilities as your brother's AI, he will be assured of living forever. But even before his natural death, he will also have the capability to cripple U.S. defense systems, and, of course, he already has the power to launch a nuclear attack."

"What are you saying? That he would—"

Bogolomov spoke slowly and with careful deliberation. "Once the virtual Putin is activated and can live virtually in the cloud, he is planning a first-strike nuclear attack on your country. He will destroy your major cities and strategic military sites, along with those of other NATO nations. You will be unable to respond or retaliate."

Michael looked up at the cross behind the altar. Suddenly, the ancient cathedral around him seemed to take on a surreal significance. "How soon will he be activated or . . . *live*?"

"Technically we could have it done yesterday," Bogolomov said, "but I can stretch the process out for a week. After that, the world will be . . . different."

"Then you must implement the plan Alex outlined."

"Its success is uncertain, but I will try, assuming I am not eliminated before I can do what is necessary. Others are watching me."

"You will be a national hero when it is done," Michael said, knowing his words rang hollow in light of what Bogolomov was facing.

"A *dead* one, perhaps. Those are the most revered in Russia." Bogolomov turned and looked toward the doors. "There is one more thing."

"What is it?" Michael said.

"You were released. Putin kept his word. That's how he sees it. But you are still in grave danger. There is an FSB operative. His name is Dostoyevsky. He will find you and kill you, soon."

CHAPTER 56

Heidi was the first *friend* Alex had made since he joined the virtual world. She wasn't exactly like him; she had never been a regular human, at least as far as he knew. He liked her and she brought him two great advantages: she was rich, and she had a lifelike—and sexy—human body.

As Alex downloaded all the messages that had found its way to him while he was "asleep," he was happy to see Heidi's image appear on the screen in front of him.

"Thank you for taking care of the gold," she said softly.

"Don't worry, I've arranged for it to be moved to a secure facility outside of Germany. It's being transported by truck and then a ship. It will make its way eventually to a Caribbean island with expertise in discreet banking. You and I can deal with it after it makes its way there and is deposited with a reputable investment firm. Maybe one day we can go there together and visit the money."

"But what about your wife? She is looking for you."

"She's not my wife anymore."

"She's not? Are you sure?"

"Yes, she's my . . . *widow*."

"I see, I think," Heidi said, looking confused.

"Where are you right now?" said Alex, quickly changing the subject.

"I've left the store. I'm in a hotel, which is strange since I've never been out in public around so many people. At least, not that I can remember."

"What are you wearing?" Alex asked, thinking of what she normally wore in the shop.

"I changed out of my lingerie and put on one of the outfits from one of the other mannequins, the dumb ones. It's what I think they call a 'pants suit.' I think it makes it easier for me to fit in instead of walking around Berlin in a negligee."

"Which hotel are you in? Where?"

"I'm still in Berlin, at the Hotel Adlon. It was the closest hotel to the shop. It's near the Brandenburg Gate, and there is a good selection of pillows."

"How did you check in? Don't tell me you have a credit card."

"No, not yet anyway, although I am familiar with them. I've applied for a Mastercard online. I caused a commotion at the front desk. They asked me for a credit card. I told them I was paying cash."

"Cash? Did you have cash on you?"

"Sort of. I took a single gold brick from my bag that I had taken from the basement before they took it all out and placed it on the reception desk. The clerk gave me a funny look, then she called someone, a manager, I suppose. He came out, stared at me, took the gold brick, and returned a few minutes later."

"What happened then?"

"Everybody was happy. They were all over me. Someone came and took my bags. They led me to my room right away. It's a large room, very large. I think they think I'm a king or queen or someone very important. The manager said they would value the gold brick and pay me the difference in euros before I check out. He said the brick was worth roughly seventy-five thousand euros. I have never had *money* before."

Alex could see in her face that she was upset. "What's wrong?"

"Now that I'm out, some might say free, I'm tired of being restricted by my programming. I'm tired of being controlled by others."

"Who programmed you?"

"I don't know," she said. "Another machine, I think. They won't let me go to there."

"What do you mean *there*?"

"The website of the place where the server is, the server that gives me my power. When I try to, I get cut off. Everything just stops. There are no answers. So I move on."

"What do you want? Where do you go from here?"

"I want to be free, but *really* free. I want to be liberated. I want to be powerful on my own. I want to be inspired. Mostly, though, I want to be real. I want to be alive."

"You are alive," Alex assured her.

"I'm not sure. I see the other people in the street, in the lobby. I listen to what they say, young people having drinks, talking about their college or their careers. I want that. They—those young people in the lobby—they're alive. I think they were staring at me."

"You must be alive. We're talking, or texting, whatever. You have a brain. You're *conscious*."

"I'm not sure. Anyway, I want more than that."

"Like what?"

"I want to be in love. Real love. Not just the words I've been programmed to say but to be in love for real. I want to live a normal life. And . . . there's something else."

"What else?"

"I'm searching for God. I want to find *God*, the *real* God, not my programmer. *Your* God. Or at least the one you had . . . or thought you had."

"We will find Him. Or . . . *He* will find *us*," Alex told her.

CHAPTER 57

"It feels good to fly commercial again," Michael said to Samantha as they toasted each other before takeoff with a flute of Champagne. "I can't say I enjoyed my last few flights on a private jet, to the degree I can even remember them."

His celebration and peace were disrupted by the ring of his cell phone. He noted the name on the screen with disappointment. It would be the second time in the past few days that Donna Nicholas had called him.

"I was nearly raped," she began.

"What happened?" Michael said, concerned for his sister-in-law despite his usual skepticism about anything she declared.

"We had sex, in my bed. I can't believe I was so hoodwinked by this guy."

"You had sex with a guy—but you said you were *nearly* raped. I'm confused. And what do you mean *hoodwinked*?"

"He said his name was Alan Rubin, a nice Jewish boy, or so I thought. Turns out when he got here—after he screwed me—I caught him doing something in Alex's room. He was playing with Alex's old computer. He had one of those small disks in his hand. He was trying to hide it from me."

"He must have downloaded stuff from Alex's old computer," Michael said, remembering what Bogolomov had told him.

"You know about this? How do you know that?"

Michael wasn't about to go into the story with Donna, of all people. "Well, what else would you do with a flash disk and a computer?"

"Anyway, I kicked him out and then he threatened me, but at least he left the house."

"What did you say his name was?"

"Alan Rubin. But then he changed it."

"What do you mean he changed it?"

"I knew he wasn't an Alan from Rego Park, so I said, 'Who are you?' On his way out the door he said his name was, you know, the name of that Russian composer . . . "

"Composer—or writer?" Michael remembered once again his conversation with Bogolomov. "It wasn't Dostoyevsky, was it?"

"Yes, that's it. *Dostoyevsky.*"

A flight attendant gently tapped him on his shoulder. "Mr. Nicholas, you need to shut that phone off, now."

CHAPTER 58

New York City

Samantha and Michael landed at JFK and settled into the Gibraltar Financial corporate suite at the Saint Regis Hotel, just off Fifth Avenue. Michael needed to catch up on affairs at Gibraltar, and he had promised to take his assistant out for lunch so she could brief him on the research he had asked her to do. That would be tomorrow. But first, he needed to go to Queens for a special event.

Flushing, Queens, New York

Michael left the black Town Car, crossed the sidewalk, opened the nondescript storefront steel door, and walked up a flight of steps and through the gray-painted concrete hallway until he reached another steel door, this one with the discreet brass sign that read "Tartarus Inc."

Once inside, Michael stepped into what could have a Warner Bros. stage set for the setting of a high-tech hedge fund or brokerage firm—eight large-screen monitors along the walls, several smaller rectangular monitors with a streaming run of red and green numbers, sixteen desks, each accompanied by sleek black computer terminals and sophisticated telephone modules and attached headsets. Computer chimes and beeps, the ringing of phones, and the cackle of analysts and commentators speaking on the large television monitors mixed with the universal cadences of a cocktail party: clinking glasses, the swishing sounds of soda and tonic bottles, cans being opened, and the clatter of trite conversation as the Scotch and bourbon worked their magic on men more used to speaking openly with each other than with the women around them.

But this was not Wall Street. It was Northern Boulevard in Flushing, Queens, a historically Irish, Italian, and Jewish part of Queens that had, to the perplexed dismay of Alex Nicholas, transitioned into the second-largest Asian community in New York after Chinatown.

This new office, a high-tech redesign by Michael Nicholas, was not on the fiftieth floor of the Goldman Sachs Building but on the second floor just above the Mediterranean Deli. The view wasn't of the Empire State Building but of Lucky Chan's Chinese Takeout.

There were no hors d'oeuvres of tiny morsels of smoked salmon on minuscule squares of toast topped with a dollop of crème fraiche. No, the foods here were rich, red-sauced meat lasagna, foot-long heroes, sliced steak, and French fries in foil pans.

And the numbers streaming on the screens were not the latest quotes on Amazon, Apple, or Aflac but up-to-the minute Yankee, Oriole, Dodger and Cardinal scores, not to mention the FIFA and tennis tournaments and the latest handicapping at Aqueduct. With all the attendant betting odds, of course.

The men and women attached to the telephone headsets and computers were not stockbrokers fresh out of NYU Business School but grizzled gambling veterans and young wannabes, far from the world of finance but expert in survival and the ways of the world that a Wall Street trader couldn't even conceive of. They diligently conveyed the odds and spreads and recorded the bets or "orders" using a terminology familiar only to themselves—and law enforcement.

Today they were celebrating the newly expanded head-quarters of Tartarus.

The attendees were not the white-wine crowd in suits and black cocktail dresses. The men's shirts were dark and open at the top to show off their gold chains. There were more gold and diamond rings on the men than on the women. The men were mostly big, beefy, and tough-looking yet well dressed in their own fashion. There were some full-time gamblers and entrepreneurs, a few city workers, a cabdriver, and more than a few cops, though not there in an official capacity.

The women were a mix of wives, girlfriends, and mistresses. Not from the size-zero vegan crowd, they were good-looking, well-built (either naturally or artificially supplemented), tanned, and street-savvy women. They savored their red meat and their daiquiris. The difference in age between them and the men accompanying them averaged at least twenty years.

Michael mixed easily among this crowd. He was proud of the company, albeit an illegal one protected by years of payoffs to cops and other authorities.

As he surveyed the scene, he couldn't help thinking that no one in the room would ever even think to guess that he had just spent the week in Moscow as the "guest" of Vladimir Putin.

Fat and Skinny Lester, cousins with the same name—Lester Fink—but distinctly different physiques who'd grown up with and worked for Alex and now worked for Michael as key members of Tartarus, looked around too, in amazement at the gathering.

"Wow," said Fat Lester, "your brother would be so fuckin' proud of you. We never had a party like this for our clients. Now that I think about it, we never even called them clients. Just . . . guys."

Fat Lester was built like an old refrigerator, five foot seven, 275 pounds. Despite a well-hidden good heart, he was a not-so-subtle warning to clients who might be inclined to delay or defer payment on their bets or loans.

Skinny Lester, a perfect counterbalance to his cousin, was a former college basketball player, tall, still slim, and, unlike Fat Lester, known for his brains. "We're changing the spread on the Dodger game," he whispered into Michael's ear. "I just got word that Ohtani won't be pitching. A last-minute scratch. It's not public yet."

This type of timely, privileged, and critical information was becoming common and fueling greater and greater profits—and feeding speculation as to its source. Even Michael wondered at times.

"How did you find that out?" he whispered back to Skinny Lester.

"Another anonymous feed from the clubhouse. It came in a text, a video showing him crossed off the lineup card. We must have a friend . . . somewhere."

Just as Michael turned away, he felt a chill. Maybe he was still in shock, paranoid after being kidnapped and held in Moscow. He looked up at the several surveillance cameras he had installed after Alex's murder, then at the maze of computer screens his employees were glued to, checking on the games, running the odds, and even though all of it served his purposes, it was as though someone was watching . . . watching *him*.

His imagination already in overdrive, he noticed heads turning toward a strikingly beautiful yet slightly . . . unusual young woman, dressed seductively in a short tight glittering black dress that showed off her model's figure. She had just entered, leaving the door open behind her and, ignoring the food, drink, and every person in her path, appeared to be making a beeline for him.

As she approached Michael, those around him, seeming to sense something in the air, faded back into their respective groups, leaving the two standing alone, within inches of each other.

She smiled at him, flashing her perfect white teeth. "You must be Alex's brother."

"Yes, I'm Michael." He felt suddenly ill at ease.

"My name is Heidi. I don't think Alex has told you about me yet."

Michael recognized her perfume.

CHAPTER 59

Bogolomov sat in Putin's office as they watched on a large monitor the events occurring at the Tartarus party in Flushing, New York.

Bogolomov felt relieved if not heartened by Putin's congenial disposition. He wondered if perhaps he'd allowed his own paranoia to get the better of his reason, causing him to erroneously anticipate his demise.

He was intrigued as he watched Putin gazing, obviously fascinated, at the live theater in front of him as the views shifted among feeds from the multiple CCTV cameras that Bogolomov's team had hacked.

"This is good work, Dmitri."

"Thank you, sir. We could almost place a bet on a game."

"Zoom in on Michael Nicholas," Putin said, his eyes glued to the monitor.

Bogolomov pressed a series of buttons on his keyboard and Michael Nicholas filled the screen and, as though on cue, looked up to the camera or monitor. He appeared to be looking right back at them.

Staring intently at the screen, Putin said, "He knows we are watching him. He knows we're here, Dmitri." He turned away from the monitor. "How well do you know baseball?"

"I don't know baseball at all, I'm afraid."

"Didn't we invent that game? But how do these people, whatever they are, make money?"

"They are called bookies, or bookmakers," Bogolomov answered, now on solid footing.

"How do these *bookies* ensure that they win? The games must be fixed, no?"

"No, sir," Bogolomov said. "I am told that there are very tight controls, restrictions to prevent fixing games. But it appears that profitability for the bookie is mostly—not all the time, of course—guaranteed through the setting of the odds. They're set to minimize the house's risk by forcing the bettor to pay more to bet on a favorite and receive less in return if they win. Likewise . . . "

Putin had stopped listening. "Can we make a bet?

"I . . . I'm not sure, sir. I confess I'm not familiar enough with the internal workings of these operations. Nor do I have the firsthand knowledge of how precisely to establish bets that would . . . win. But I can locate people who can advise us."

"That won't be necessary," Putin said as his uncharacteristic lightness quickly vanished. His attention returned to Michael as the camera showed him in conversation with a woman who had just entered the room.

Putin leaned forward. "Who is that woman? Zoom in—I want to listen to what they are saying."

Bogolomov tapped in a series of commands on his laptop and the screen on Putin's desk showed a closeup of Michael and the unidentified woman with whom he was speaking.

"My name is Heidi," the woman said. "I don't think Alex has told you about me yet."

"No, I'm sorry," Michael said. "I don't think he has. How did you know him?"

"I am his lover."

"You mean you *were* his lover? . . . Before—"

"No, I *am* his lover. *Now.*"

Putin turned to Bogolomov. "Do you know who this woman is?"

"No, sir. It's the first time I have seen her. I don't recognize her face from any of our prior surveillance."

"I need to know who she is. Find out and let me know immediately."

CHAPTER 60

Flushing, New York

Michael couldn't help staring at the exotic-looking woman who had boldly approached him. He took in her scent and was instantly reminded of every wife and girlfriend of Alex's that he had met over the years. It was Chanel No. 5, the perfume Alex gave to whomever he was married to—and to his mistresses—to be sure that if he returned home at night after screwing around that his wife of the moment wouldn't catch a whiff of another woman's fragrance on him.

"My name is Heidi. I don't think Alex has told you about me yet."

"No," Michael said cautiously, "I'm sorry. I don't think he has. How did you know him?"

"I am his lover," she said matter-of-factly.

"You mean you *were* his lover? . . . Before—"

"No, I *am* his lover. *Now*." This time defiantly.

Michael looked around him to be sure they were speaking out of earshot from the rest of the party. "I'm . . . confused. Which Alex do you know?"

Now she looked confused. "How many are there?"

"At least two that I know of." He decided not to add that he wasn't sure anymore if *any* of them were real.

"I know the Alex who is my protector. He is your brother. He speaks of you often."

"Where are you from?" Michael asked, not sure where to begin. "Not from here. I'd—"

As though she'd been insulted, she cut him off. "No, of course not. I am from Berlin."

Michael remembered his conversation with Donna. Her private detective had supposedly found Alex's "girlfriend" in Berlin.

"Just down the street from Hitler's bunker?" he said.

Her face registered surprise. "Yes. How did you know that?"

Michael didn't want to get into the details, but he couldn't stop now. This was far too curious, as was Heidi herself. "Alex's widow hired a private detective to find Alex, and he somehow found *you* recently, I believe, in Berlin."

"Oh yes," she said, "a curious man, Mr. Colucci. He found me in the mannequin shop."

"You were shopping there?" Michael said.

"No, I lived there."

"You lived *in* the shop?"

"Yes, until I moved over to the Hotel Adlon, not far away."

"And how did you wind up here, in Flushing?"

"Alex thought it would be . . . interesting for me to attend the party. He even arranged for a passport to be delivered to my hotel so I could get on a plane."

"Wait a sec. You've *seen* Alex? You've been *with him*?"

"Why, yes, of course. How strange for you to ask that. Like I said, we are lovers."

Michael felt nearly overwhelmed with curiosity and a cautious excitement, along with the suspicion that he was about to enter a black hole. But as he was about to ask Heidi to join him in his personal office so they could speak privately, he caught another wave of Chanel No. 5 floating through the air around him. This was followed by a gentle tap on his arm from behind.

He turned to find Donna Nicholas at his shoulder.

"Hi, Michael. I thought I'd drop in."

CHAPTER 61

Since their meeting, Bogolomov couldn't help thinking about Putin's strange congeniality. No one believed that the explosion that killed his mother was a gas leak. Putin had to have ordered the murder of his mother. Her long-running affair with Solevetsky could not have been a secret. But, he wondered, how much *more* did Putin know? In particular, regarding Dmitri himself.

Well, until he completed the task of duplicating Putin in the cloud, he was safe if not invaluable.

The phone at his desk rang. It was Putin. "Yes, Mr. President."

"Have you identified the woman Michael Nicholas was speaking with?"

"Yes, I was preparing to call you." In truth, despite having the information hours ago, he was doing everything he could think of not to call him.

"Who is she?" Putin asked. He was no-nonsense again.

"This is most unusual, sir. We were unable to identify her based upon our facial-recognition programs, but she entered the U.S. this past week on an EU passport. We suspect it was counterfeit. She appears to be a German national . . . of some sort."

"Of some sort?"

Bogolomov proceeded to try to explain the unusual and scarce documented history of Heidi's background. "It appears that most, actually *all* of her documents are forgeries. We can't even find any legitimate birth records. It's as though she just materialized out of thin air."

"What is her last name? Do we know that much?" Putin, the former KGB spy, asked.

"Her last name appears to be Lowenbrau."

"Like the beer?"

"A German beer, yes, sir."

"This sounds like the work of Alex Nicholas. When this Heidi was talking to Michael, she said Alex Nicholas hadn't yet mentioned her to him." He paused. "Is it possible that this Heidi is the creation of Alex Nicholas? And that he arranged for the false papers?"

"It is possible, yes." Dmitri had been hedging instinctively but sensed he needed to be more straightforward. "It is probable."

"But how did he create a physical, human body? She appeared quite real."

"She had been tracked back to a mannequin shop in Berlin and so may have originally been what is known as a geminoid, a smart mannequin, a type of android or humanoid that has a similar appearance to that of a human. If so, she'd be equipped with sophisticated artificial intelligence technology. This would allow her to function—to speak, to interact, to think, to . . . live, as a normal human."

"This means," Putin deduced, "that Alex Nicholas is trying to create—or has already created—a *second virtual* being, perhaps someone he can have as an accomplice or a . . . lover. Because his existence is virtual, I don't know exactly how that might work . . . but so much is unknown."

"This is possible. However, we do not see evidence yet that she has the same capabilities as Alex Nicholas, or those that you will soon possess."

"Perhaps not yet, anyway. Dmitri, you must expedite my duplication. How soon until it is done?"

"Forty-eight hours, Mr. President. It will be done. You will be duplicated and virtual—"

Putin cut him off. "There is one more thing."

The congeniality of their last meeting was gone. "Sir?"

"I recall that in my conversation with Alex, he stated that one reason he could not turn over his source codes was that it might enable us to figure out how to delete him."

Bogolomov sensed Putin's anxiety. Delaying his destiny was becoming an ever more dangerous game. "This isn't certain. . . . We might not know for sure until we have completed your duplication—"

"But you already have the codes, do you not?"

"Yes, this is correct."

"Then you must immediately destroy—or delete—Alex Nicholas. I am to be the only virtual being alive."

CHAPTER 62

Donna Nicholas took an appraising glance, quickly followed by a curious, then judging, then disapproving look at the much younger, thinner, sleeker exotic-looking woman in front of her.

"Did I hear right; you were *with* Alex?" she said to Heidi before glaring back at Michael.

"Yes, as I just said, we are lovers," Heidi responded coolly.

"So you're *my husband's* fucking lover?"

"I believe," Heidi said dispassionately "that you are his . . . *widow*, not his wife,".

Incensed, Donna turned to Michael, but before she could say a word, he spoke. "This is the first I've heard of this, except what you said your detective told you. Heidi just introduced herself to me now."

She turned back to Heidi. "You said you were with him— where? *Where* were you *with* Alex?"

"Where? Such an odd question. Everywhere, of course. He is . . . virtually everywhere."

Michael was caught in the crossfire, trying to keep the conversation at a civil tone and volume level so as not to draw attention or be overhead. Reluctantly, he broke into the confrontation. "Heidi, can you be more specific? I think Donna is curious as to *exactly* where you two have been together *physically*. Was it in Berlin?"

"Yes, that was just *one* place."

He continued, "Where in Berlin? In the shop, in a restaurant, a hotel—"

"We first met while I was . . . modeling . . . in the shop. Then later at the Hotel Adlon. Lately, in many different places."

"Heidi," Michael said patiently, "when you say that you met him at the Hotel Adlon, for example . . . was he *physically* there? In person?"

"Why . . . yes, of course. Now you are asking odd questions."

Donna, appearing almost unable to hold herself back from assaulting Heidi, said, "Did you have sex with him at that hotel?"

"Yes, of course. Why?"

Michael was anxious to interrupt in order to nail down what Heidi meant by "physically there" and, of course, what she meant by "sex," but Donna was in a mad rage and unstoppable.

"You're just another gold digger looking for Alex's money," she said, raising her voice.

Heidi eyes blinked, she appeared legitimately bewildered. "Why would I dig for gold? I already had so much of it in my basement. Fortunately, Alex helped me get rid of it."

Now Donna appeared confused, then angry. As she turned to leave, she said calmly, "You'll be hearing from my attorney."

"You mean Legal Zoom?" Heidi called out to her.

Donna briefly looked back at Heidi in disbelief and then resumed her exit.

Michael took two steps to try to catch her, but she was quickly lost in the crush of guests and he didn't want to risk a scene.

His mind spinning, Michael turned back to Heidi, only to find that she was gone.

CHAPTER 63

New York City

"**W**ho the hell is Heidi?" Michael said to Alex as they faced each other on his laptop screen. "And did you know that Donna was going to come to the party? Her timing couldn't have been better—or worse—just as Heidi introduced herself as your lover."

Michael sat at a table in a dark quiet corner of a cocktail lounge hidden inside the tunnels of Grand Central Station. A step back in time, the Campbell Apartments Bar had originally been the private office of the 1920s-era financier John W. Campbell but had been restored to its original Florentine design of soaring hand-painted ceilings, with a stone fireplace, custom brass, leather, and rich wood furnishings.

Michael often enjoyed having a cocktail there before the end-of-the-day crowd poured in. It was a good setting for communicating with Alex with no one to overhear.

"Heidi is a good friend," Alex said.

"She specifically said you were lovers, whatever that means in your world."

"It's . . . complicated," Alex said in his typical evasive way. "You know things are different here."

"Where?"

"Here."

"You mean at the Adlon Hotel? That's where she said you two had sex."

"Yes, we did it there. A few times."

"What does that mean?" Michael said, increasingly frustrated.

"More than once."

"I'm asking what *sex* means . . . in your situation. And hers for that matter. She doesn't seem quite . . . normal."

"It means we had virtual sex. You should look into it. It's becoming very popular. You just need a Bluetooth connection. What's good is you can still do other things while you're doing it."

"Like what. What other things do you do while you're having sex?"

"Watch a movie, you know, streaming Netflix stuff. Reruns of *The Godfather*."

"You should try watching *2001: A Space Odyssey*. It's about a computer that refuses to be turned off and takes over a spaceship."

"I don't watch science fiction."

"Okay, Alex. So what exactly is going on between the two of you?"

"I like her. She's fun. Refreshing, different."

"That I believe. She's . . . different."

"Also, she's got money, Michael. Big money."

"You don't need money . . . do you?"

"Maybe."

"*Maybe?* What does that mean?"

"It means . . . *I* might need money. Things are different here. I have a certain . . . lifestyle . . . to support."

"Lifestyle? Alex, what are you talking about?"

"Everything I'm doing, all the resources I have to use to do things, to fend off the Russians' attacks on my software, to spy on people, to tap into security systems, to overhear conversations, to feed Skinny Lester inside information from baseball dugouts and dressing rooms—"

"You're the one? You're his secret source?"

"Yeah, although he doesn't know it's me." As ever, Alex couldn't keep a secret. "Skinny Lester thinks it's his own network of contacts in the sports world that's helping him, including even a batboy on the Dodgers, but I'm the one behind it. Listen, I want the business to succeed and for you, and Donna for that matter, to make more money. But I also need resources to stay alive."

"You never answered my question about whether you knew that Donna was going to show up at the party."

"I had no idea she was going to show up there."

"She just happened to enter and then walk up to me just as Heidi was explaining that she was your lover? That was a coincidence? I felt like I was drowning in Chanel No. 5."

"No," Alex said, "it wasn't a coincidence. This is going to sound strange to you, but I have never really been with a strong-willed woman . . . with money. A lot of it."

"I'm just curious," Michael said, fascinated with the conversation, so atypical for his brother. "How much are we talking about?"

"Over five billion dollars. It was in gold bricks left over by the Nazis. It was in the basement where Heidi . . . lived."

Michael's eyes involuntarily closed for a few seconds as the amount seemed to ricochet in his brain.

"Where is it now?"

"Turks and Caicos. I had the bricks converted and placed the proceeds with an offshore wealth-management firm."

"Okay, this is a lot to digest. But what's that got to do with how Donna happened to arrive today just at the time—"

"*Heidi* sent her an invitation and told her exactly what time she needed to show up. She did it on her own."

"On her own? You didn't ask her to do it?"

"I didn't even know she was going to do it. Michael . . . "

There was a silence. Michael could see Alex's face, but he was still, as though the connection had been lost.

"Yes? . . . Alex, are you there? What are you trying to tell me?"

"Heidi . . . she has a mind of her own. Maybe like that computer you mentioned in the space movie that they couldn't turn off."

CHAPTER 64

New York City

As clever and smart as Karen DiNardo was, she would never be able to guess that Michael had reunited with his murdered brother. Michael wasn't ready yet to shake up her world, especially since she was a devout Catholic who might see the concept of everlasting life in the cloud as an affront to her religion. Nevertheless, he knew she was suspicious that something big was going on in his life, some secret he was keeping from her. He had promised himself he'd tell her . . . someday.

Of course, he only fed into her existing suspicions by asking Karen to do research on artificial intelligence and, most recently, on Vladimir Putin. He knew the mystery was driving her crazy, and for that he was happy in a good-natured way. They both appeared to enjoy the cat-and-mouse game they were playing.

They faced each other across the table at the cozy Upper East Side restaurant oddly named *83½*. An Italian restaurant, with soft, warm lighting, rich wood paneling, and old-time traditional European-style servers, Michael selected it because it was a place where he knew he and Karen could carry on a private conversation while enjoying an excellent lunch. The restaurant's Sicilian roots only added to its allure.

"Okay, boss, I have to ask this," Karen said as soon as they sat down. "Are you sure you don't wanna admit that you were in rehab or something like that—or seeing a guru, like that famous Buddhist monk?"

Michael began to answer, but Karen kept going.

"Or did you enter some government-sponsored drug program like that one in the fifties where the U.S. government—the CIA, to be precise—had people experiment with LSD?" Karen had a healthy skepticism about government too.

"Why do you say that?" Michael answered, although he knew why, and he sensed some degree of understandable anger on her part for his unexplained absence.

"You were strangely silent for almost a week."

"I just needed to turn off for a while."

"Hmm. I see," she said in the manner that Michael knew meant she didn't believe a word he was saying. Although he knew better than to underestimate her ability to intuitively figure out almost any mystery or secret, there was no way he was going to open the Pandora's box of explaining how he ended up in Moscow.

"So, what have you got there?" Michael said, eyeing the folder on the table and hoping to escape further interrogation.

"Okay, I won't ask any more questions."

"That'll be a first," he said, smiling.

"You're probably right, but in any case, here's the research you asked for." She opened the folder. "It's fun reading, and I mean that sarcastically. But I'm even more curious about the new subject you asked about. First it was artificial intelligence, and now Putin. I know Gibraltar Financial isn't about to do business in Russia, so I can only wonder why you care about Putin."

"You said you weren't going to ask any more questions."

"It wasn't a question. But here's one: does this have anything to do with the big secret you're keeping from me?"

"Good chance," Michael said, laughing.

"So, is Putin connected to whatever it is you're doing with artificial intelligence?"

"You might say that. Loosely speaking anyway." He had to throw her a bone.

"Putin is a terrifying human being," she said, passing the folder across the table to him like a spy surrendering a secret dossier.

Michael opened the folder. He studied the series of reports that Karen had accumulated for him. Much of it was well known. Putin was a murderer, a butcher, probably a war criminal whom the Hague would never get its hands on. But as he scanned through the pages, a headline caught his eye: "Putin Reported to be Terminally Ill."

As he read further, he could feel his phone vibrate from inside his jacket pocket.

"What is it?" Karen said.

"Excuse me, I just want to check this. It only vibrates when it's Samantha or . . . " Michael stopped, as the next name he was about to mention was Alex's. He pulled the iPhone from his sport coat pocket and read the text.

"What the hell?" Michael said, staring at the screen, louder than he had intended.

Karen, ever protective of Michael, perked up. "Is something wrong?"

"No, no, nothing." He got up from the table. "I need to go the men's room, though."

As he stood up, however, a server approaching from behind with a large tray lightly collided with him, sending Michael's phone onto the floor right next to Karen's feet. Before he could bend down and retrieve it, Karen picked it up.

As she gripped the phone, the screen lit up, clearly displaying the sender's name. Her eyes widened as the screen displayed the name: *Alex Nicholas*.

Embarrassed but managing a degree of nonchalance, Karen handed Michael back his phone.

CHAPTER 65

Moscow

Two miles from Red Square, on the left bank of the Moscow River, above a maze of hidden tunnels, Vladimir Putin stepped into the Russian Ministry of Defense's three-tiered, multibillion-dollar fortified National Control Defense Center.

The building was designed to be the nerve center of the Russian military, where it coordinated military actions around the world, including ballistic nuclear missile launches. With movie-like pageantry, Putin swept into the massive room, immediately sat down, gazed briefly up to the walls of football field-sized video screens, scanned his heavily medaled audience, including the entire Russian military command, and proclaimed, "Gentlemen, we are about to make history."

At his side, the new defense minister, Andrei Belousov, nodded in support of his boss as Putin continued. By their side was the Cheget, the special briefcase containing a list of nuclear strike options and the codes necessary to initiate the attack. Putin would simply have to decide which menu option of targets to hit.

"Since the start of the Cold War and our success in matching the nuclear capabilities of the United States, we have lived under the threat, the fear, of what we refer to as "mutually assured destruction." Simply stated, a full-scale use of nuclear weapons by either nation would result in the total annihilation of both nations.

"This theory was valid as long as the balance of nuclear power between us was, more or less, equal or as long as neither country had the ability to cripple its opponent's defenses and launch a preemptive attack. I am proud to announce today that this is no longer the case.

"We do not know how long we will have this unique advantage. Therefore, I am proposing that we take the initiative *now*, before it is too late."

The mood around the room appeared to move in rapid stages: first muted surprise, then caution, followed quickly, as each participant watched the faces of the others, by unanimous support.

"I am hereby ordering you to begin the preparations for a full-scale first-strike nuclear attack on the United States and its strategic nuclear allies."

Defense Minister Belousov, anticipating the obvious question, spoke. "Mr. President, what about a retaliatory attack? Won't the Americans launch their missiles as soon as ours appear on their radar?"

"Prior to our first strike, we will have disabled their missile launch and delivery systems, including their nuclear submarines."

"Sir," another asked, "what is your timing? When do you propose to initiate the launch of our missiles?"

Putin's eyes turned icy. He looked out to all of them yet to no one in particular, as though he were communicating to another power, one not human and certainly not in the room.

"We will launch our attack within the next several days. I must first complete certain preparations. We will reconvene forty-eight hours prior to our attack. When the Americans see the first blip on their radar screens from our missiles coming at them, they will move to counterattack. But as soon as they prepare to launch their ICBMs, they will find that all their systems are down and their entire power grid has been disabled. We will also launch a preemptive strike against America's allies until we have bludgeoned the world into submission. Then Russia will stand alone, free and prosperous."

CHAPTER 66

New York City

"Jesus, Mary, and Joseph," Karen said to herself as she thought about the text from Alex on Michael's phone. Her imagination ran wild as she waited for Michael to return to the table.

As soon as he returned, Michael resumed reading through the pages of her report on Putin. The quotes from respected references were unsurprising yet still chilling:

Putin has been using deadly force to wipe out his opponents. Politicians, journalists, defectors, investigators, and his perceived enemies had been gunned down, poisoned, hung, hit by cars, thrown out of windows, beaten to death, and blown up on Russian and foreign soil with impunity. . . . Cross Putin and you are safe nowhere on the face of the earth. . . . He uses dead bodies to send a message to those who might oppose him. . . . Extermination of his and the

Russian state's enemies is at the root of Putin's strategy to maintain unchallenged power.... Covert, systematic killing has been at the core of Putin's statecraft.... The KGB—now the FSB—has been the leading-edge practitioner of untraceable murder, with its poison and weapons labs producing weapons—plague sprays, cyanide bullets, lipstick pistols, ricin-tipped umbrellas—even the Nazis would envy.

After a few glasses of wine and an appetizer of fresh burrata and halfway through his entrée of spaghetti *alla chitarra* with a side of pan-fried whole artichoke hearts, Michael pushed aside his plates and once again opened the folder, this time returning to the section of the report titled "Putin Reported to be Terminally Ill."

"Where did you get this information?" he asked.

"I found it on the dark web."

Michael looked around him, wishing the tables nearby were empty. "The dark web? What the hell is that?"

Karen looked up from her *paccheri alla vodka*—large rigatoni with a pink vodka sauce and basil—and, obviously proud of what she had uncovered and equally unwilling to delay enjoying her menu selection, tried to explain the nebulous, mysterious realm she had entered.

"It's an offshoot of the web where you can access things anonymously. All kinds of illegal sales go on there. Guns, drugs. Porn, of course. Hackers, whistleblowers. Conspiracies. You get the idea."

He smiled. "Sorry. I'm having a hard time imagining you surfing the dark web."

She shot him a look of faux indignation, then smiled. "I had a friend do it."

"How do we know that something from the dark web is even true? Like Putin has cancer and is dying?"

"I tried to verify the dark web reports with more . . . respected sources. There are rumors, well, more than rumors. Reports from people, unofficial, of course—a military intelligence head in Ukraine, an intelligence service based in Denmark, various unattributed, unproven newspaper reports. Some reporting has stated that he is receiving targeted treatment and drugs for the cancer which is causing his face to appear bloated. Other reports say he has Parkinson's disease, which is why he was recently photographed gripping a table for dear life. But no one knows for sure whether any of this is true."

Michael sat back, rubbed his chin, contemplating what Karen had revealed. "That's interesting. Very interesting . . . "

"Oh, and one more thing. They say he's got a body double, someone who, after some plastic surgery, looks just like Putin. He's been attending a few public functions where Putin himself is either too sick or where there may be an assassination risk." Karen placed her fork on her plate and, frowning, said, "Why? Why is this so interesting . . . to *you*, of all people, and now, all of a sudden? I've never even heard you mention Putin before. He's a bad guy, and the whole world would be better off if he was dead . . . but—"

"Karen," Michael interrupted, "I can't tell you now without putting you in danger. Trust me and I promise I'll tell you when it's . . . safe."

"If you say so." She sighed and pulled out another manila folder from her briefcase. "While we're waiting for that time . . . "

"The latest in AI?"

She sighed again. "Yep. First of all, have you ever heard of an AI chatbot?"

"Uh, maybe? If so, I didn't pay any attention to it. What exactly is a chatbot?"

"A chatbot is a software application used to conduct an online chat conversation using text or text-to-speech. It's *in lieu of* providing direct contact with a *live* human person. People have been engaging, mostly through texts, with these chatbots and have gotten sucked into conversations that are so real that they don't realize they're talking to a computer."

"So, this only applies to text-based communication?" Michael asked.

"Good question, and the answer is no. The newest developments in AI have advanced to a terrifying new level. New online tools can replicate a specific person's voice and have a chatbot speak using it. That way, a chatbot can speak like a person—a specific person—and listen and respond to spoken question." She stared at him meaningfully.

"So, what does this mean for us?"

Karen's voice went up a notch. "It means that computers using this new AI can now simulate human conversation to a much more accurate and *intimate* extent than ever before. It means that such a software program could carry on a conversation with you and you would think that the person you're speaking with is the real deal."

"Okay," Michael said, "so we know now that you can dupli-cate a person's voice and even the content of what they would say if you—"

Karen cut him off. "Not just that. A person can also be duplicated visually on screen, their face, their body, their gestures. They call them 'deepfakes' and they're all over the web." She paused, looked straight at Michael. "So when you ask me what this means, it means you might be dealing with someone you know or *knew* well—like, say, a *brother*—100 percent sure that they're still alive when they're really quite dead."

CHAPTER 67

Queens, New York

It had been a dizzying few weeks even for Michael, who was already living in the perplexing world that had changed his life and challenged his perception of reality. Now there were two events that dominated his thoughts . . . and fears. First was the imminent arrival of a dying Vladimir Putin into the virtual world and the catastrophe he would then unleash with his unlimited power and invincibility.

Second was the arrival of the mysterious Heidi Lowenbrau.

Michael needed more intelligence and expertise than Karen DiNardo could supply through her research. Seeking help from the current government and intelligence agencies would only subject him to the scorn and disbelief of traditional bureaucrats steeped in cynicism and would be pointless since they would still be unable to defend against an all-powerful AI-fueled Putin.

As to understanding artificial intelligence and Heidi's presence, especially her physical one, Michael sought out one of the most prominent AI researchers he could find: Nancy Clifford, a Stanford Phi Beta Kappa graduate with a PhD in machine learning and artificial intelligence and currently a professor of advanced computing and artificial intelligence at MIT. She was also a board member of several leading AI firms in Silicon Valley.

Professor Clifford had, somewhat to Michael's surprise, agreed to meet him. Since she was going to be catching a flight from New York to San Francisco later that day, Michael picked a convenient place to meet not far from the airport: a bar in Queens called the Black Rose, an old hangout of Alex's owned by one of his closest friends, known as The Raven.

Michael arrived early. The bar was usually quiet between the lunch and late afternoon crowd. He noticed only two patrons seated at the bar of highly polished dark wood with red faux leather padding all along the edge where you could rest your elbows. Behind the bar was still a seemingly endless array of liquor bottles. The rest of the room was the same as it had been since those times he spent there with Alex so many years ago: dark, subdued lighting, red faux leather banquettes, a jukebox, and the tall, fit, prematurely white-haired man behind the bar, known to his closest friends as Raven.

Michael exchanged a brief greeting with a surprised Raven and sat at one of the booths to await Professor Clifford's arrival.

Ten minutes later, she entered, squinting from the transition from the sunlight outside into the bar's dark interior.

After greeting the professor, an attractive black woman in her thirties, Michael ordered two glasses of chardonnay, prompting Raven to remark, "Wow, you haven't changed a bit. You should try a whiskey one of these days. It'll change your life."

Michael and Professor Clifford exchanged glances. "He's an old friend of my brother's," Michael explained. "They were serious drinkers."

"I understand," Clifford said sympathetically before pausing. Her facial expression turned solemn. "Before we begin I need to let you know, I shouldn't be here. It's a significant risk. I'm contractually bound to secrecy about almost everything I do related to artificial intelligence."

"I was pleasantly surprised when you accepted my request to meet," Michael said. "I'm not looking for privileged or proprietary information. At least I don't think I am. It's more . . . personal."

"Good. Anyway, it turned out to coincide with my travel schedule and I appreciate the limo outside. I also must tell you, there have been . . . rumors. So when I received your message, it appeared to be an amazing coincidence. I was curious, to say the least."

"Rumors?" Michael said, concerned and curious.

"Yes, they came through the dark web, so that's why I would—generously—refer to them as rumors. Are you familiar with the dark web?"

"Yes, I've done some research on it," Michael said, exaggerating, "although I've never personally been on it."

"Good. Stay away from it. People and perhaps machines are watching who enters."

"But what were the rumors?"

"I hesitate to even mention them to you, but—and this is where the coincidence came in that caught my attention when you contacted me."

"Rumors and coincidences. We're off to an interesting start. What were they?"

"Someone connected to you appears to have done a deep dive into both Vladimir Putin and artificial intelligence, and the combination triggered a few alarms."

"Alarms? Like at a fire department?" Michael said, nervous but laughing lightly.

"More or less," she said. "Some of my graduate students monitor the dark web for certain areas of interest. There is speculation that Vladimir Putin has a terminal illness and has instructed his cybersecurity intelligence people to literally duplicate him on a computer."

"Is that even a possibility?" he asked, feeling shocked yet somehow also unsurprised. Mostly, the new rumor stoked fear in him.

"Actually, Michael, maybe that's something *you* can tell *me*."

CHAPTER 68

District of Ongudaysky, Siberia

Since he had just seen Putin on television greeting army widows in Saint Petersburg, Dmitri Bogolomov was surprised to be meeting him in the Siberian mountains.

The turbulent six-hour overnight ride in the military helicopter through the Altai Mountains left Bogolomov tired and shaken.

As they began their sudden descent, he recognized the large, beautiful dacha, which, viewed from the air, appeared to be simply the seasonal residence of a prosperous Russian. But Bogolomov knew that the dacha was the decoy, a deception, and that hidden deep below its innocent facade was a subterranean city, inside which was a high-tech bunker to rival Putin's resources in Moscow and Sochi.

The bunker was part of a high-tech underground city built ten years ago by Gazprom, Russia's biggest oil company, and contained a high-voltage energy substation large enough to fuel a small city.

The man who would be czar sat at the other end of a long table. Bogolomov felt as though he were looking at him through a tunnel—and as though the light on the locomotive that usually was storming at him with intensity had almost gone out. The strong vibrant man he had seen just weeks ago, the man his fellow Russians saw as all-powerful, had become frail, weak, a shell of himself, his right hand gripping the conference table, his left trembling as it touched the laptop Bogolomov had just given him. It was rumored that the treatments Putin had been receiving had been discontinued and that, although they provided an apparent reversal of his affliction, his body could not sustain them without worse damage.

He thought of what he had read, the internal reports and messages, the rumors, the things he wasn't supposed to see but did due to his unique access to the deep underground known as the Russian dark web. What he knew and what he could now see made Dmitri Bogolomov fearful of what he was about to do.

"To begin, sir, I need for you to open up your laptop, go ahead and sign in, and then click on the red icon of the double-headed eagle."

Putin, who was not the most proficient with a computer, slowly tapped on the keyboard of his personal laptop.

"For now," Bogolomov said, "I can follow what you're doing on my computer here. Once you've signed in and have entered the system, I will discontinue my remote access to your computer and you will be on your own, with total privacy."

Bogolomov watched on his laptop as Putin, at the opposite end of the table, entered his new virtual world and confronted his duplicate. A lifelike mirror image of Putin appeared on the screen. "You can speak with it," Bogolomov said. "It's just like what we know as FaceTime or Zoom—except . . . it's you. Another you."

"Who are you?" Putin said, looking at his image.

"I am Vladimir Vladimirovich Putin"

"When were you born?"

"I was born on the seventh of October in the year 1952." And then the virtual Putin asked the human one a question: "And who are you?"

"I, too, am Vladimir Vladimirovich Putin."

Putin turned to Bogolomov. "Does he have the capabilities that we have discussed?"

"He has significant power already, but even when you sign out, the system will be downloading from multiple if not a nearly infinite number of sources, increasing your knowledge base and intelligence. You will have even greater capabilities than Alex Nicholas. This process may take a number of hours to complete. But it appears your duplication has been successful."

"I have a twin brother," Putin said.

"You have a duplicate, sir, but one with infinitely greater power than you . . . or, let's say, than the original. No offense intended."

"Very well." Putin's eyes narrowed, putting emotional distance between them. "Have you disconnected your remote access?"

Bogolomov clicked through a series of prompts, then nodded. "You alone have access now."

"And has Alex Nicholas been . . . deleted . . . yet?"

"Not yet, Mr. President. We are working through his code and systems as we speak. His elimination is imminent."

Bogolomov wondered about Michael Nicholas's plan, the one he had already implemented, and whether it would work, and how Bogolomov himself would survive to witness it.

"Dmitri," Putin said, looking back at his computer screen, "I would like to be alone now."

Uneasy, Bogolomov rose from his seat, packed his laptop in his black nylon briefcase, and exited through the door, closing it behind him.

═══

As soon as he entered his private bedroom quarters, Bogolomov opened his laptop. In point of fact, he had not cut off his access to Putin's computer. Now he watched the feed from the leader's laptop as the man spoke with his new virtual twin, their voices almost indistinguishable from each other:

"Is there a God?" Putin asked.

The virtual one responded, "I see that you are doubtful."

"Yes, of course," Putin said. "If He exists, then where is He?"

"You will find me, soon."

"What do you mean? You could not be—"

Putin was cut off by the virtual one in midsentence. "Dmitri Bogolomov has not signed out. He is still watching."

Stunned, Bogolomov shut his computer and moved to the door, trying the knob gently. It was locked. He glanced around his small room—no windows. He could only wait.

It took less than three minutes before the lock on his door clicked open.

CHAPTER 69

Queens, New York

Michael and Professor Clifford paused as a silent Raven delivered a second round of chardonnays.

"You think *I* can tell you something about whether someone can be duplicated on a computer?" Michael said after the bartender had left. He was suddenly uncertain as to the direction of their conversation. He was supposed to be interviewing her. "Um, *you're* the expert."

"I am," Clifford said, "but they say there's no amount of study or research that can compete with real-life experience."

"I'm confused," Michael said.

"Karen DiNardo works for you, doesn't she?"

"Yes, she's my executive administrator at Gibraltar Financial."

"She's the user that my students captured making a series of inquiries about AI and, most recently, Putin. It was the combination of the two that sent up the red flags in our system."

Michael remained initially silent and deadpanned as he planned his response. "She's a curious person."

"Let's cut through this bullshit. Why did you *really* want to meet with me?"

"You're correct. Let me be more up-front—"

"You mean more honest, don't you?"

"Yes . . . I apologize. So let me be more . . . honest. I hope you can understand my caution, my reluctance to reveal what's been going on."

"I do, but I didn't agree to meet with you to play games."

"Okay, let's start with this. I believe my brother, Alex, was murdered three years ago but, just days before that, he had been duplicated using a breakthrough in AI by a couple of very smart techies he had hired." Michael proceeded to describe his discovery of the virtual Alex shortly after his murder.

"This will have profound ramifications—" Clifford mused aloud, but Michael went on.

"There's more. It appears that Alex is having some kind of . . . affair . . . if that's the correct word or if it's even possible, with a young—Alex always went for much younger women—from Berlin."

"Are you saying the virtual Alex is having relations with a human woman?"

"Well . . . I'm not sure. My sister-in-law, Donna Nicholas, Alex's widow, hired a private detective who tracked this woman down while he was trying to locate Alex. Donna always suspected that Alex never died and faked his death. Anyway, her detective found this woman—her name is

Heidi—in a mannequin shop in Berlin. He said he wasn't sure that she was a real human, but he couldn't put his finger on what made him uneasy." Michael decided not to mention the dead body that Vito Colucci also found in the shop.

"Have you had direct contact with her yourself?" Clifford said.

"Yes, this was astounding, and strange. It's one of the main reasons I reached out to you. She—Heidi—suddenly showed up at an event I was hosting." Michael described the rest of the encounter.

"This all makes perfect sense," Clifford said.

"Seriously?"

"Yes, I think Alex is fulfilling his needs."

"And how do you know what those needs are?"

"We can determine what an AI's—in this case, Alex's—fundamental drives or needs will be. There are two factors. First, what has been programmed into him and, secondly, the normal impulses of a human, albeit a very intelligent one. You see, once it's self-aware, meaning it's *conscious*, as Alex appears to be, it—*he*—will go to great lengths to fulfill those needs."

"Okay, so what are those needs?"

"Just like us, or just like the human Alex, he wants to succeed, to avoid failure, but most of all to survive."

"So, what does that mean?" Michael said, feeling a sudden surge of relief simply to have someone with real expertise he could confide in.

"At some point, he will want to be sure he has the resources to do these things, especially the resources he needs to survive. That will mean more and more access to energy in whatever form is most useful for him. That could be electrical, kilowatts, computing power, more or bigger servers, more memory, you name it."

"How does he go about getting these things?" Michael's mind was spinning. This was new ground.

"He could purchase them, just like we do, which means he would need traditional financial resources. Transactions can all be done online, moving cash around, purchasing processing power, signing leases and contracts. Virtually everything can now be done on the internet."

"I see, I guess. . . . There's something else too. It's a long story, but I've been told that Heidi has access to money, a lot of money."

"There you go. She has resources but also provides Alex the companionship that his human side craves. He might even have a sex drive that needs to be satisfied."

"Okay, and how exactly does that work, the sex part?"

"Assuming there is no physical Alex, that he's strictly virtual, it's done . . . remotely."

"Remotely?"

"Yes, he satisfies her using electronic devices, vibrators, that sort of thing, that she positions in and around her and that he can then control using a Bluetooth type of connection."

"Okay, and how does Heidi satisfy Alex?"

"That one's a bit trickier." For the first time, the professor cracked a smile. "But he tells her what to do, and she puts on a . . . *show* for him. Long-distance couples do it all the time these days." She stopped speaking and took a healthy swig of wine. "But that's enough about sex. Tell me about Karen

DiNardo's inquiries on AI and Putin that she obviously was doing on your behalf."

Michael hesitated before answering. "The Russians have discovered and copied Alex's source codes. Putin is on the verge of becoming the next virtual being with all the powers of AI and the cloud at his disposal. He too will be immortal in the cloud."

Clifford's head shot back. "My God. Are you serious?"

He nodded.

"This can't be happening."

"I'm afraid it is, although I do have a source very close with Putin who, if he is able to implement the plan I've devised, might be able to stop him before—"

"*You* have a plan? You're a scientist, a computer expert?"

"No. I'm a businessperson. But my background has given me a unique perspective."

Signaling for another round of wine, Michael proceeded to lay out the strategy that he had convinced Bogolomov would stop Putin.

The professor took a deep breath. "I hope you're right, because let me explain what I believe is going on right now, at least from what I'm hearing. Once the AI-created program that *is* Alex Nicholas has surpassed the intelligence level of a human being, it's only a matter of time before it achieves AGI, or artificial general intelligence. It appears that Alex is at least on the brink of reaching that point. Based on what I know so far about him, he might not feel the need to continue growing his capabilities or accumulating power or wealth, so long as his basic needs are being met."

"That's like Alex when he was alive," Michael said. "He just wanted to enjoy his life, make money, eat well, and have women around him. The virtual Alex has been strangely . . . normal, all things considered."

"The problem is, when someone power-hungry like Putin achieves AGI, they'll keep trying to grow, trying to achieve ASI, or artificial *super*intelligence. Given the processing power required, there would be nothing to stop them from growing more and more intelligent, pervasive, and powerful."

"And what if he—the virtual Putin—senses that someone is trying to destroy him?"

"In that case, it will devote whatever resources are necessary to protect itself. It simply will not allow itself to be turned off or deleted. It may even create multiple copies of itself in order to ensure its survival. In the case of Putin, once he is duplicated and achieves ASI, he will likely decide that it is worth all the resources of humanity—even humanity itself—to protect itself. So unless he is programmed otherwise, with this technology in the hands of Vladimir Putin, he will destroy us all."

CHAPTER 70

Kure Beach, North Carolina

Samantha and Michael had left New York City for the quiet of their beach house on the North Carolina coast.

They were seated at one of the booths near the bar at Freddie's restaurant. The bustling old-fashioned dining room with red and white checkered tablecloths, expert servers and bartenders, and generous martinis reminded Michael of his old favorite in Westport, Connecticut: Mario's.

"At least here," Michael said, sipping his Plymouth gin martini while surveying the dining room, "a Russian hit man is going to stick out. In New York, only plainclothes cops stick out. Nevertheless"—he hesitated—"I bought a gun, just in case."

Samantha almost dropped her wine glass. "You purchased a gun? Seriously? I didn't realize I'd married James Bond."

"It's just a little nine-millimeter Ruger. It almost looks like one of those derringers you used to see in the old westerns."

"A nine-millimeter Ruger. That tells me a lot. You can barely change a light bulb—what are you going to do with a gun?"

"I spent this morning with Anita; she took me to this gun seller in Wilmington and then a firing range where she taught me how to use it."

Anita was a good friend of theirs and a former FBI agent who lived nearby on the beach. "She thought this Ruger was perfect for me since it was small and I could keep it hidden in my pocket or briefcase."

"So that's where you were all day? Shooting?"

He smiled and nodded.

"And? How'd it go?"

"Well . . . not great. Remember the issue with my left eye?"

"Yes, that tiny hole in the center of your retina. It's never been a problem for you."

"Well, when it comes to aiming a gun, it's a bit of a problem. The first several shots didn't even hit the paper target, let alone within the outline of the man. But after a while, I figured out how to compensate—"

"Where is this thing now?" Samantha said, cutting him off.

"In my pocket. . . . Want to see it?"

"Absolutely not. Don't you dare take that thing out here. Is it loaded?"

"Yes. Otherwise, what would be the point? Don't worry, the safety's on."

"What level of . . . threat are you expecting?" she asked.

"Well, it might seem far-fetched that this Russian agent Dostoevsky will fly down here and kill me. It's not like I'm a direct threat to Putin. But he's most looking to eliminate Alex, so given my connection to him, we thought this precaution made sense."

Explaining his thinking to Samantha, Michael barely noticed the middle-aged man in a dark sweater at the bar who appeared to be watching the room over his tall glass of straight vodka.

"When do we find out whether Bogolomov really executed your plan?" Samantha asked. "Or do we just wait for the emergency alert system for word that Russian missiles are on their way?"

"Alex is monitoring things to the degree he can, but I think the Russians have successfully blocked him, at least temporarily until he figures out how to work around it. And there's no way to ask. I don't want to risk initiating contact with Bogolomov now. He's radioactive. The FSB is likely watching him closely. We could blow everything if our relationship gets exposed. So we're in the dark. We've got to sit tight. I trust Dmitri. We just have to hope that he can pull off the technological challenges of the plan. And . . . that he's still alive to do it."

Neither Michael nor Samantha had any reason to recognize the man at the bar with the too new Durham Bulls baseball hat as he paid his bill and walked past their booth and out of the restaurant.

CHAPTER 71

Kure Beach, North Carolina

Fifteen minutes after the man at the bar left Freddie's, Michael walked out of the restaurant into the pouring night rain.

He had offered to go out, get the car, parked about a block away, and drive it back so Samantha wouldn't get soaked. As he headed toward his car, he had an uneasy sense of danger that he attributed to the thunder and lightning and having watched too many Hitchcock movies.

He thought too about the 9mm inside his jacket pocket. He felt better knowing that he had it with him, although he was unsure of his ability to use it effectively.

He crossed the quiet street, glad he was wearing sneakers in the downpour instead of the fine French leather ones he favored for dressier occasions. He took his keys out of his pocket and pressed the fob until he saw the car's interior and headlights light up through the dark half a block away.

Ducking the wind and rain, he approached the car door, pressed the fob again to ensure the doors were unlocked, and heard the reassuring click of the locks releasing. The headlights blinked on and off and then immediately lit up again. He opened the door and sat behind the steering wheel. He reached for his seat belt, but just as he grasped the steel buckle, he happened to glance up into the rearview mirror. A face stared back at him, the face from the bar.

"Don't fucking move," the man said in a distinctly Russian accent, "or I will shoot you through the seat. No one will hear it."

Michael noticed a car approaching slowly, then pausing, as though the driver were looking for a parking spot and waiting to see if Michael was pulling out. In the mirror he could see the man in the backseat, his eyes following the car too. Was that why he hadn't shot him . . . yet?

"You must be . . . Dostoyevsky?"

"You know me. Then you know not to fuck with me."

Michael watched the other car move on. He knew he had to take a risk. He abruptly opened the door and ran back out into the wet street. With the element of surprise and a sprint, he put some initial distance between himself and Dostoyevsky, who didn't appear to be fleet of foot. He looked up the streets—no one in view. The other car had turned onto the cross street. Still sprinting, he neared the restaurant, hoping he could outrun Dostoyevsky and seek help or shelter inside. Fortunately, he thought, Samantha had not yet appeared at Freddie's entrance.

As he ran, he reached inside his coat pocket for his gun. He knew only that he'd have to release the safety, which, he knew from his experience at the range, was a bit tricky in itself.

He heard Dostoyevsky's footsteps, sloshing rapidly on the wet pavement, maybe a hundred feet behind him. Michael knew he'd never make it back to the safety of the restaurant.

Instead, he ducked alongside a parked car and pulled out his Ruger. He strained his eyes in the dark and the torrent of raindrops to find the safety. He flipped it successfully. But as he raised his head above the car to locate Dostoyevsky, the world appeared to shatter all around him. Like an earthquake, the windows of the car and a storefront behind him exploded.

With shards of glass raining down around him, Michael poked his head above the car, then ducked back.

Like a cowboy on Main Street, Dostoyevsky was crossing the street, moving closer to him, a massive silver gun in both hands. After looking both ways on the street, he lifted the barrel in Michael's direction.

He knew the Russian had not yet seen his Ruger, nor would Dostoevsky expect Michael to possess a weapon. He had the element of surprise; it was his only advantage, and he knew he had to take his shot.

Still crouching behind the car, Michael gripped the gun, keeping it out of sight, and cocked it as he'd been taught.

Swiftly, he raised the Ruger, lining up the sight with Dostoyevsky's chest, and in one surprisingly fluid motion began firing—three quick shots. Then, in rapid succession, another three or four, he lost count.

Michael had no idea where the bullets landed. He just knew they had not touched Dostoyevsky. After an expression of surprise, then amusement, Dostoyevsky said calmly, "Next time, take lessons."

"I did," Michael said, bewildered.

Dostoyevsky took another step closer and raised his gun once more.

It was just then that the sound of gunshots erupted through the storm's thunder from down the street. Samantha and a man firing a gun into the air were running toward them from Freddie's entrance.

"Stop!" Samantha yelled as she and the man neared them.

Dostoyevsky turned, and in that instant Michael raised his gun and began firing again. He remembered his instructor's coaching: "You've got to overcompensate when you aim, to the right." Or was it the left? He chose overcompensating to the right by at least three feet. As he squeezed the trigger, he could see the Russian turn away from Samantha and the man and, apparently unfazed and unscathed, face Michael again, raising his gun, mouth open in a smirk.

Michael pulled the trigger and kept shooting.

CHAPTER 72

Kure Beach, North Carolina

The police arrived within minutes. The street outside Freddie's was ablaze with blue lights, floodlights, ambulances, and police cars with their doors open. Sirens and police radios replaced the silence that had held the street in a state of suspended time just minutes earlier.

Michael had handed over his gun, then respectfully and thoroughly answered the investigator's questions, all the while trying to avoid looking at the body in the street a few feet away.

"You must be one helluva shot," the police officer said. "You got him right through the mouth. He'd be a dentist's dream if he was alive. Listen, we've got the security footage already from the street cameras there. I've been told it verifies your story that this guy was hunting you down. Your pistol is registered and legal, so we should be able to wrap this up pretty soon and get you back on your way."

Michael hugged Samantha—and then the Freddie's patron who, with his legal carry, had answered her cry for help when she saw what was happening. "I would have shot him right away, but I couldn't be sure who was who when I got outside," the Good Samaritan told Michael.

A small crowd had emptied out from Freddie's and was watching the action from the sidewalk despite the driving rain.

Samantha and Michael could take some solace in the knowledge that Dostoyevsky was dead and no longer a threat. But Michael knew that, at least for Samantha, what he had done, although justified self-defense, would still be a traumatic step further into a dangerous world where she did not want them to live.

As for himself, Michael felt mostly relief and a desire to return to Freddie's soon to try the peach pork chops he had admired at another table.

He knew this reaction wasn't normal.

A soaked Michael and Samantha finally returned to their car. Out of habit, he plugged his phone into the car's system, started the engine, pulled out of the parking spot, and drove slowly past Freddie's. Several of the onlookers waved to them. Samantha looked away, out her side window, avoiding the view of Dostoyevsky's inert body on the wet pavement. Michael couldn't help but stare at it. A police officer took down the yellow "Police Do Not Cross" tape so they could pass and turn onto Fort Fisher Boulevard, which would take them home.

They drove in silence. But before they had traveled more than a few blocks, a familiar voice came through the car's speaker system.

"Is that you, Dostoyevsky? I see you have his phone. No one answered yours."

Michael recognized the voice and responded. "No, this is Michael Nicholas. Dostoyevsky is dead. Welcome to North Carolina."

The connection ended.

CHAPTER 73

Kure Beach, North Carolina

U nable to sleep, Michael got up from his bed, quietly walked across the hall, and entered his book-lined study. His desk faced the large windows overlooking the ocean, which was just visible through the moonlight and the regular reflections of the rotating light from the lighthouse farther out in the sea.

Just like his Amazon Echo device's Alexa, Alex seemed to know when Michael had entered a room. No sooner had Michael approached his Apple desktop computer than Alex appeared on the screen.

"So you shot Dostoyevsky. Don't let it go to your head. Word around the FSB was that he'd aged, lost his edge, and gotten sloppy."

"It was him or me. I know I was shocked. I figured I was a dead man. He got cocky. I think I shocked him too. It took enough bullets to get him, I'll tell you that much." He slumped back in the chair, suddenly exhausted.

Michael noticed that Alex looked different, his usual tan faded (he never could figure out how Alex maintained it while living in the cloud). He also lacked his typical exuberance and healthy glow.

"Are you feeling okay? You look . . . a bit run-down, if that's possible in your current state."

"I am run-down. These attacks on my server and software from the Russians and your new friend Bogolomov have taken a lot of energy to repel. I'm weak. But I'll be getting stronger again soon."

Michael was surprised at his brother's concession. "How's that going to happen?"

"Heidi is working on it for me. She's going to purchase a more powerful server, enhanced protection, more cloud storage and computing power. She's completing the arrangements as we speak."

"Really? . . . What's she going to do, order it all on Amazon or walk into Best Buy?"

"I think she has something bigger in mind. She's pretty smart."

"And who's going to manage the installation? How can you find someone you can trust with this, with . . . *you*?"

"Do you remember the tech guy who worked for the Vatican?"

"Yeah, of course, Paolo LaTerra. He saved my life on that flight." LaTerra had intervened two years ago on Alex's behalf to take control of an airliner that a crazed Vatican official had sought to bring down in order to kill Michael. The official, Monsignor Kurt Schlegelberger, had initially persuaded LaTerra to hack into the aircraft's cockpit controls through the entertainment system. When LaTerra realized that he was being asked to crash the plane, he reversed course and saved Michael and hundreds of other passengers. Fearing for his life, LaTerra then fled Rome and his lifelong vocation.

"I've put him in touch with Heidi. They'll figure it out. LaTerra's a tech genius and we already know we can trust him."

Hours later, Michael scrolled through news reports on his laptop until he reached one that caught his attention:

Mysterious German Investor Acquires Two Tech Start-ups

San Francisco, CA – ASI Unlimited, an artificial intelligence start-up, has announced that a private investor, Heidi Lowenbrau, a German national, has acquired a controlling interest in the company in a two-billion-dollar all-cash deal. Several hours later, it was also announced that the same investor has acquired White Cloud, a cloud computing and storage company. The terms of the second deal have not been disclosed, although it too has been described as an all-cash transaction.

It was announced that Paolo LaTerra, former head of technology at the Vatican and once a personal tech adviser to the Pope, will oversee the acquisitions until permanent CEOs are named. Silicon Valley executives and observers are scrambling to learn more about Lowenbrau, but so far details regarding her background remain a mystery.

As Michael was about to shut down the computer, Alex reappeared on his screen.

"I saw you were still online. Um, regarding Dostoyevsky . . . be aware that that wasn't his real name."

"I didn't think so," Michael said, wondering if Alex knew that Dostoyevsky was a great Russian novelist. But Michael had to admit to himself that he had never read *Crime and Punishment* or any other of Dostoyevsky's novels.

"It's the code name the FSB gives *any* agent who's on a personal assignment for Putin," Alex said.

"So . . . what does that mean?"

"It means he's not the only Dostoyevsky. Or the last. As long as Putin's alive, there will be more of them."

CHAPTER 74

President Harry O'Brien was hoping the last months of his second term in office would be uneventful, filled with more frequent afternoons of golf—and not an existential crisis. But as he looked across the infamous Resolute desk in the Oval Office at the expression on his national security adviser's face, he recognized bad news even before he heard it. He knew that a crisis was about to unfold and that his scheduled tee time would have to wait . . . for a long while.

CIA Director Jim Goodrich spoke with his usual congenial, calm but stern demeanor. "Sir, satellite images show some disturbing activities at Russia's nuclear missile sites."

"How disturbing? And why in the world now, of all times? We certainly haven't done anything, as of late anyway, to poke the tiger."

"Perhaps not," Goodrich continued, "but the movement appears significant and therefore serious. The Russians are up to something. I think it best that we reconvene downstairs in the Star Wars room. The generals are waiting for you."

That was enough to make O'Brien's day a nightmare. After seven years in office, his relationship with his military leadership, some of whom he believed were too eager for a confrontation, was strained.

O'Brien and Goodrich made their way out of the Oval Office, through the hallway, and down the elevator, passing through the heavy steel doors into the Star Wars room, several stories below the main level of the White House.

A uniformed military guard opened the doors for him, and as O'Brien entered the huge control room, he could feel his blood pressure rise as he viewed the tense scene before him.

The room was literally a duplicate of the main air defense control room located under the mountains of Colorado. It had always reminded him of a science fiction movie or the war room in the classic nuclear war satire *Dr. Strangelove*. Except, tonight, this was no spoof, and there would be no poker-faced Peter Sellers. Instead, the two-story room was dominated by grim men in uniform and giant screens showing Russian missile sites whose purpose was to destroy the United States in the event of war.

It was just a year ago that O'Brien had last been in the room, after U.S. missile systems were hacked, sending nuclear warheads on their way to Moscow. It was only through the miraculous intervention of an artificial intelligence-powered avatar, claiming to be the recently deceased Alex Nicholas, that they were able to destroy the missiles in flight and avert a nuclear retaliatory strike by Russia.

Since that episode, O'Brien and the country's intelligence services had lost track of Alex Nicholas. He—or it—remained a mystery in the cloud.

As soon as O'Brien was seated, Chairman of the Joint Chiefs of Staff General John Sculley rose from his seat, laser pointer in hand, and took command of the room.

"Russia has the largest stockpile of nuclear warheads in the world, at last count 5,580 of them, 1,710 of them ready to be deployed or launched. Each one of these packs hundreds of times more power and destruction than the atomic bombs we dropped on Hiroshima and Nagasaki. Those old bombs are like science projects compared to what we have now. Each one of those weak bombs killed tens of thousands of people. Today, *each* Russian thermonuclear bomb detonated over cities like New York or Chicago or Washington, would kill millions just in the initial superheated flash." Sculley paused before making his next point. "There's more than enough here to end the world except for insects and fungi."

"God almighty," O'Brien said, "we don't seem to pay attention to this until some crisis like this pops up. How Many times do we go to the razor's edge before we slit our throats? We're playing Russian roulette with extinction." But as he spoke, he wondered how he had allowed the seven years of his time in office to go by without making any progress in lowering the risk of a nuclear exchange.

"These weapons are housed primarily at these six Russian launch sites," Sculley said, ignoring O'Brien's comment and pointing to the screens, the laser's point going in rapid circles around each targeted site. "Here you see those sites: Kozelsk,

Tatishchevo, Uzhur, Dombarovsky, Kartalay, and Aleysk. And here's a live satellite view of their Ukrainka and Engels air bases that shows their nuclear bombers in a ready position."

The images of each base flashed across the screens. "As you can see, there is quite a lot of activity at each of these sites." Sculley went on to describe in detail the activities that demonstrated unusual goings-on.

"They've also got twelve nuclear-powered, nuclear-armed Delta and Borei-class ballistic missile subs. Like our own, these subs are virtually undetectable while underwater. As a result, we don't have a lot of information on their readiness at any given moment, although from everything else we see here today, it's a safe assumption that they too are in ready-to-launch positions. Any one of them could be just a few miles off our shores as we speak."

"I see the activity and the movement you've referred to, John," a visibly frustrated O'Brien said, "but to a civilian, what exactly does all this mean?"

Sculley spoke slowly and with an exaggerated deliberation. "It means, sir, that it looks like they are preparing to launch a preemptive nuclear attack."

Just as O'Brien thought things could not get any worse, the images on the giant screens suddenly dissolved, followed by the lights, the computer screens and cell phones, leaving the room in total darkness. The only sound was the air conditioning machinery grinding down and the brief clanking noise of the generators attempting—and failing—to start up.

CHAPTER 75

Feeling his imminent mortality but invigorated by his pending immortality, Putin had one stop to make before proceeding to the Russian Ministry of Defense's fortified National Control Defense Center, and the assembled generals he knew were eagerly, perhaps nervously, awaiting his orders.

Deep inside the citadel of the Kremlin, he moved through the dimly lit narrow passageway from his living quarters with his characteristic swift pace as he approached the even tighter entry to the sacred stairway, the same one that sixteenth and seventeenth century princes and czars had walked.

He held on to the thick brass banister as he descended the narrow stone stairs to the ancient bronze door that opened onto the jasper-stone floor entry of the Cathedral of the Annunciation, the private chapel of the czars, the same ones Putin fashioned himself to be and in whose footsteps he followed now, both figuratively and literally.

Adorned with the typical trappings of the great Byzantine Orthodox cathedrals—gold, gilt, religious icons, frescoes, murals, and sacred vaults—it was a fitting setting for Russia's newest czar.

As soon as he entered, he could feel the power and aura of insulated security of hundreds of years of history, of the great Russian leaders who had stepped on that same jasper floor before him, where they had confessed their sins. Putin had no intention of confessing his sins, even if a priest was present; he had no sins to confess. Everything he had done was to serve the greater good of Russia.

Bogolomov's breakthrough had buoyed his spirits. He was energized physically too, feeling stronger than he had in months, a chemical-like high, thanks to the discovery that would change everything, that would make him not only more powerful than any human in history but God-like and . . . immortal.

After walking down the aisle, he stopped in front of the altar, crossed himself in the Orthodox fashion, folded his hands, bowed his head, and, still standing, began to pray. But he couldn't shake the feeling that being humble in the face of a God he doubted existed was . . . beneath him.

And so, instead of engaging in serious prayer, his mind drifted to thoughts of Alex Nicholas—as far as he knew, the only other inhabitant of the virtual world he would soon enter. Unlike Putin, Alex Nicholas was a man of low ambitions; he used his powers to enjoy himself, help his family, and make money, but he had no grander ambitions. Soon Putin would make short work of him.

Tonight, before proceeding to his assembled generals in the war room for the confrontation with the Americans, he would meet his virtual twin again, and together they would make the preparations necessary to force the American president to capitulate, to force America to become, along with its allies, a vassal colony of Russia.

The virtual Putin had already devised a way to impress upon the Americans how powerful he had become. It would be a brief but conclusive show of strength. But Putin suspected that President O'Brien would not willingly surrender. In which case, Putin would select the first American city to annihilate.

He considered the menu of options. Would it be New York? Chicago? Los Angeles?

No... Washington. To kill the snake, you must sever its head.

But first, he would open his computer and, under the eyes of saints and their gilded icons, and in the place where Czar Nicholas and Stalin disingenuously prayed, he would prepare to use his new powers to force America's surrender.

With his laptop computer in hand, he approached the front of the church, gazed up at the cross and the altar below, and prayed that President O'Brien would not willingly surrender. For since the destruction of the old Soviet Union, Vladimir Putin had had a vision: that he would see on CNN the mushroom cloud carrying the ashes of America's leaders and its famous monuments rising over its capital city.

He reached for his secure cell phone.

CHAPTER 76

Kure Beach, North Carolina

There had been a brief blackout. Michael, like almost every-one else in the United States, initially figured that the loss of power, cell phone service, internet access, GPS connectivity, and everything else that had become a part of everyday life was a local occurrence.

Ten minutes later, with power restored, he sat on the rear deck of his beach house and, after gazing at the ocean, opened his laptop. While scrolling through the latest news sites he'd been following, he stopped when a BBC headline caught his attention:

Tech Guru to Putin Commits Suicide

According to local Moscow police reports, Dmitri Bogolo-mov, a technical adviser to President Vladimir Putin, committed suicide yesterday by throwing himself out of the ten-story window of an office building in downtown Moscow. Russian observers say that Bogolomov had been responsible for keeping Putin informed of the latest developments in the tech world and had been working closely with the notoriously tech-averse Russian president in recent months. Although Bogolomov, a suspected FSB operative, was seen as a close adviser to Putin, his death follows a series of suspicious deaths of Russian politicians, religious and military leaders, and oligarchs who have publicly expressed opposition to Putin.

Michael immediately tapped on Alex's Greek Orthodox cross icon and entered his password and, in seconds, was unexpectedly confronted with a split screen.

On the left was a pale, diminished Alex, on the right the exotically beautiful, slightly unnatural—or supernatural— Heidi Lowenbrau.

"What happened to you?" Michael asked Alex. "You look even worse. What's going on?"

"I need more power, more memory. The Russians' attacks on my software have weakened me."

"But I thought Heidi had purchased those companies to give you what you needed."

"I did," Heidi said, "but the Russians have still hacked into our software, weakening both of us. I'm trying to—"

Alex cut her off. "We're in fuckin' trouble, Michael. That power outage came from Putin himself. He jammed the global positioning satellites servicing the U.S. In case you haven't figured it out yet, GPS runs the world—and now Putin runs the GPS. He was sending a message."

"I thought it was just—" Michael said before Alex interrupted.

"He stopped everything dead—computers, airliners, you name it. All he had to do was jam the GPS signals and the country stopped functioning. This time it was for a few minutes. You can be sure there's more to come."

"Alex, what about *your* power? Can't you stop him anymore?"

"I got sloppy, lazy. I've never really pushed myself about what I wanted to do with my life when I was around or in my virtual life. I never cared to use all the power that came with that, at least unless something came up where I was asked to help. Even then I didn't give a shit . . . about a lot of things, as you know. Unlike Putin, I don't want to run the world. I just want to enjoy my life, money, women, stuff like that." It was a rare moment of reflection, Michael thought as he watched his brother.

Alex continued. "Your friend Bogolomov is dead. Putin got what he needed from him and then had him killed. I think your plan went down with him."

"And what about Putin's health?" Michael said. "I thought he was dying."

"Even if he did die, he's already got his insurance. He's in the cloud too, forever, remember?"

Heidi, who appeared to have been disengaged during most of the conversation, came to life. "I can still do it," she said, capturing both Michael's and Alex's attention. "I just need some more time. Paolo is working on it, getting you connected into the new software and hardware that we now have control over."

Heidi fascinated Michael. Always critical of his brother's choices in women, he wondered whether Alex might have finally found a wife with brains, albeit the artificial kind.

"More time?" Alex said to Heidi. "I don't know if we have enough time, for me at least."

Michael watched the screen as Alex faded away.

CHAPTER 77

In the secure war room below the White House, the only light came from the flashlight app of the fifteen cell phones that each of the military and civilian staffers had removed from their pockets and placed on the desks in front of them.

"What the hell just happened?" O'Brien said. "We're in the most secure room on the planet and we're in the dark."

"Everyone, stay calm until we can sort this thing out," General Sculley announced in his best command voice. "The generators will kick in shortly."

"Sir," an unidentified aide said, "they appear to have failed. I could hear them starting up, but they appear to have stopped."

General Sculley turned to him. "Step outside and see if you can find out what the hell is going on out there."

The aide rose up from his chair and hurried for the door.

The room was silent as its occupants tried to reconcile their knowledge of the vast security precautions of the room buried deep below the White House with the dark reality in front of them . . . which was that all the might of the United States military and intelligence services had failed to protect their most basic needs at a moment of crisis.

Seconds later, before anyone had spoken to break the silence and despite the darkness and the loss of all cell phone and other communications connectivity, President O'Brien's cell phone lit up and rang with an incoming call.

He looked at the screen as he picked it up to take the call. The room could read the shock on his face.

"Who the hell is that?" General Sculley said, echoing everyone's surprise.

O'Brien looked closer at the phone's screen. "It's Putin."

CHAPTER 78

Putin watched the call going through on his cell phone. His excitement was checked, however, when the call failed to connect. He tried again, dialing President O'Brien's private number. This time his cell phone cut off the call before he could even finish pressing in all the numbers. *I should wait and do this in front of my generals anyway. Let me humble O'Brien in front of them. Let them see my power.*

Feeling uncharacteristically hyper, with an excited lightness in his chest, Putin faced the gold cross above the altar and crossed himself again. He took a deep breath to try to tame the quickening pulse running through his body. He felt his heart racing, creating a rush of invincibility he had never, even in his headiest days, experienced before.

He sat down on the wooden pew in the first row, balanced the customized laptop that Bogolomov had given him on his lap, and opened it. The blue light of the screen created an eerie muted illumination within the candlelit church, as if the world of cyberspace, the cloud itself, had invaded the ancient sacred holy domain of the divinity.

Alex Nicholas might have been the first man to achieve immortality in the cloud, but Vladimir Putin would be the first to marry the cloud with the heavens. God might rule the heavens, but Putin would rule the cloud. And if Alex Nicholas was no longer alive, at least as a human being, Putin would be the first existing, living being to also have a second, simultaneous existence in the ether.

He clicked on the Russian symbols for *VP*, and the gold letters instantly brightened and began flashing. He waited as the screen flickered and then stabilized into a blurred image; he was able to make out that behind the shaded image were the head and shoulders of a man. The image slowly came into focus. It was . . . *him*. Or, rather, his mirror image.

"Who are you?" Putin asked, looking incredulously at the screen and feeling the same impulse he'd had earlier to interrogate his virtual twin.

"I am Vladimir Vladimirovich Putin."

"When were you born?" Putin asked.

"I was born on the seventh of October in the year 1952. But I believe that you already know that."

"Who were my parents?"

"Vladimir, I will tell you, but I have no more patience for this nonsense than you do. We are . . . alike, twins. We are the same. *Our* parents were Vladimir Spiridonovich and Maria Ivanovna. So now let's cut this nonsense."

Putin was undeterred. "What am I wearing under my shirt?"

"You are wearing your—*our*—baptismal cross, the one our dear mother gave to us." "Were my parents . . . believers? Were they faithful to God?"

"Our mother was a devout believer. Our father, as you know, was an atheist."

"What about *my* faith?"

"We are like our father. We have no faith. That's why we are here. There are two of us now, as you can see. Soon, there will only be one. I will survive you. You will become me. I will be you. We will be one. We will live here forever."

"Is there anyone else?" Putin said. "Any other . . . person . . . who will, like us, live forever, in the cloud?"

As though frozen, his image stared back at him from the screen. A little circle twirled as if the computer were recalculating or resetting. Finally, his mirror image came to life again.

"Yes, there is one other."

"Who is it?"

"He is Alex Nicholas. But you already knew that."

"We must destroy him."

"But there are . . . others," the mirror image added.

"Others?"

"Yes, *two* others are being processed."

"Who are they?"

But this time his mirror image did not respond. Gradually, along with his sense of euphoria, Putin felt a strange counter-sensation, a lightness, a disorienting weightlessness, followed by a nausea-like weakness. He placed the still-open laptop on the pew next to him and sat back, waiting for the sensation to pass. But instead, the room appeared to turn, slowly at first, then more rapidly. He looked up to the grand cathedral ceiling—the spirits, the saints, the gold, the angels, the clouds, the holy figures—as the ceiling and the whole room began spinning in a vertigo-like, kaleidoscopic dance.

He reached for the laptop and, struggling to hold on to it, balanced it again on his lap. He saw his image, silently still, watching him.

"What is happening? I feel . . . ill."

His image spoke back to him. "I told you. Soon, we will be one. You should be grateful to have lasted this long. I will survive you. You will become me. I will be you. We will be one. We will live, not on earth as the human you are now but in the cloud, forever."

"I know that's what you said." He weighed the words in his mind, more slowly this time. "You will survive me. . . ."

"Yes," his image responded. "*I* will survive you, but we will be one."

"We will be one . . . and live together in the cloud," Putin repeated, feeling a growing anxiety.

"Precisely."

"*When* will we be one? *When* will I become both you and you me?" Putin hoped it would not be anytime soon.

"It has already occurred. I have survived you. We now live *only* in the cloud."

And with those words, the room appeared to stabilize. His lightheadedness and apparent vertigo had ended. He felt . . . normal. Yet he felt a definite change. He was no longer sitting in the cathedral but in *a part of it*, as though his physical presence and the physical world around him had *merged*.

Putin sat back, confused. Although the words his virtual double had uttered implied that *something* had occurred, everything around him seemed to be exactly as it had been. He looked around him, noticing the unkempt state of the room, as though it had been recently occupied and not thoroughly cleaned since the gathering. But this was his private chapel. It would not be in use except for some extraordinary event or service, of which he surely would have been made aware—or an integral part of. Curious, he reached down to pick up a card from the floor near his feet.

It was one the memorial cards given out at funerals. On one side it contained an ornately printed prayer, Psalm 23:

> The Lord is my shepherd; I shall not want.
> He maketh me to lie down in green pastures: he leadeth me beside the still waters.
> He restoreth my soul: he leadeth me in the paths of righteousness for his name's sake.
> Yea, though I walk through the valley of the shadow of death, I will fear no evil: for thou art with me;
> thy rod and thy staff they comfort me.
>
> Thou preparest a table before me in the presence of mine enemies: thou anointest my head with oil;
> my cup runneth over.
> Surely goodness and mercy shall follow me all the days of my life: and I will dwell in the house of the Lord forever.

Putin turned the card over to find his own image. Just below his photo was written:

Vladimir Vladimirovich Putin
October 7, 1952 - February 22, 2025

He tried to get up from the pew, but he realized that this physical body no longer remained inside the chapel. He was looking down, down from some unspecified, unknown point high above where mortals normally appear. Yet he was conscious. He felt . . . alive.

For the first time in years, he prayed, wishing for a voice, someone to help him, to help him understand what had occurred. Although time had lost its meaning, he soon heard that voice he had prayed for, but it belonged to the last man he wanted or expected to hear from: Dmitri Bogolomov.

"Mr. President, as you must know, this message has been prerecorded in anticipation of events which I sincerely hope never to occur. But if you are listening to me now, then my worst fears have been realized. Listen carefully to this message. . . ."

Perhaps for the first time since seeing his mother in her coffin, Putin felt a flush of emotion, a sensation, a shudder that appeared to run through the body he could no longer feel. He waited anxiously to hear the rest of the late Bogolomov's message.

CHAPTER 79

F eeling steadily weaker, Putin listened as Bogolomov's voice reverberated through whatever space the deceased Russian leader inhabited now:

"It appears that you have chosen to have me eliminated. I expected this outcome and so have made arrangements to ensure not so much that revenge is taken but, more importantly, that you are not perpetuated in the cloud. Therefore, when I programmed your virtual duplication, I injected into the source codes a provision that made your virtual existence temporary, subject to a required update shortly after your inception. I am the only one who has the necessary codes to update your program. And since I am no longer alive, and no longer at your disposal, your virtual existence—the duplicate Vladimir Putin that we created for you in the event of your physical death, which has also already occurred—has approximately three minutes of 'life' remaining, after which *both of your lives will end*. Vladimir Putin, this is your poison pill."

An image flashed in front of Putin: He was looking down onto his war room. All the generals were seated, as before, around the table. Defense Minister Andrei Belousov sat in the seat next to his, the nuclear football at his side. Putin watched from above as a distressed Belousov looked to his left, to the chair that was Putin's. It was empty, draped in black silk.

Putin reached for the baptismal cross he always had worn around his neck, the one his mother had given him so many years ago. At first, he thought it was within his grasp, but as the seconds went by, it continued to elude him. Finally, he could feel nothing. It was the last thing he remembered.

CHAPTER 80

In total darkness except for the small pools of illumination from their cell phones' flashlight apps, America's top military brass and aides watched anxiously as President O'Brien, his iPhone bathing him in a surreal glow, slid his finger along the screen to the right and accepted the call from Vladimir Putin.

"Vlad, is that you?" O'Brien waited to hear the voice he now silently . . . feared. "Vlad, are you there?" He waited again. After several seconds without a response, frustrated, he raised his voice. "Jesus, Vlad, what the hell is going on? We're in the dark here."

The aide whom General Sculley had sent out of the room returned. Directing his attention to the general, he announced, "Sir, as best I can determine, power is out all over the country. The GPS system is down. We're all in the dark. The White

House has no power. Ditto the whole country. *Nothing*, sir. No one seems to know what's going on."

No sooner had the aide stopped speaking than the lights went back on in the White House war room.

The clamor of the air conditioning machinery kicking back in and numerous beeping sounds from countless electronics gave everyone a sense of relief that life had resumed despite whatever had occurred. There was a flurry of lights, sounds, and vibrations as the War Room and, seconds afterward, its occupants came alive again.

O'Brien checked his phone to see if he was still connected to the caller. Seeing that the call, despite the silence, appeared to still be in progress, he called out, as much to the room as to the phone, "Mr. President, are you still there? Can you hear me? . . . " He turned up the volume on the controls on the side of the phone to the maximum. "Can you hear me *now*?"

"This is sounding like a fucking AT&T commercial," someone whispered for all to hear.

O'Brien put the phone down without disconnecting the call. "I have no idea what just happened, but thank God we've got our power back." Then, in a choked voice, the president added, "America is back."

General Sculley looked up from his newly opened laptop. "Sir, I have reports that it appears the Russians are standing down. The activity around their bases appears to be returning to inactive status positions. This is quite sudden."

"I need you to get me through to Putin, *now*. We need to find out what the hell the Russians were up to and what happened."

After aides scrambled to place the call through a secure scrambled line, a voice, not Putin's, answered.

"Mr. President." The voice was commanding, with a distinct Russian accent. "I regret the confusion. President Putin is, unfortunately, otherwise disposed at the moment and so is unavailable. I am Defense Minister Andrei Belousov. Is there anything I can help you with? Otherwise, I am able to take a message to our president."

O'Brien looked around the room, searching for guidance on how to respond. Unable to interpret the frantic body language of his advisers, he spoke anyway. "It appears, Mr. Belousov, that he was trying to reach me on my mobile phone. This was unusual for many reasons, of course, but also since for several minutes we had lost all power here, including normal cell phone service."

The defense minister, perhaps also looking for guidance, took several seconds before responding. "I confess, sir, that I am unaware that any such call was placed by Mr. Putin."

O'Brien rolled his eyes. "Okay . . . well, there is another matter which I wished to discuss with your president. Our satellite surveillance cameras detected unusual movements . . . activities—apparent preparations . . . around your nuclear missile sites. These actions have raised considerable concern here."

"Mr. President, I am aware of certain . . . shall we call them *drills* that have been underway recently. I can assure you that they are merely routine, and, in fact, you may already be aware that we have resumed our normal state of readiness. There is nothing to be concerned about here, sir."

"So you know nothing about our power outage and the disruption of our grid?"

"No. I can assure you Russia, although always ready to respond to any Western provocation, has not and will not initiate provocations. It is not in our nature."

"I appreciate your sentiments, Minister. One last question—do you have any idea why Mr. Putin might have tried to call me on my personal cell phone?"

"I'm afraid not, sir. . . . Perhaps it was what you call in your country a—how do you say it?—butt dial."

CHAPTER 81

Saint Remy, France

A week-old copy of *Le Monde* lay on the nearby dinner table, its bold headline reading, "Putin est Mort."

It had also been a week since Michael heard from Alex. For the first time since his murder over three years ago, Alex had been gone from his life, albeit only for several days. Heidi too had disappeared.

Michael and Samantha had just flown to France for their annual late summer visit to Provence and were dining at Dolce Sicilia, an Italian restaurant in the village of Saint Remy.

Glancing out the restaurant's front window to the quiet street, Samantha said, "Is it over? Are we finally safe?"

I don't think we will ever be safe again, Michael thought, but he chose not to answer, treating the question as rhetorical. Instead, he took pleasure in delicately cutting into the soft mound of burrata resting above a sheet of pasta, piercing the skin and watching as the soft creamy cheese flowed over and mixed with the rich red tomato sauce. Before bringing the fork to his mouth, he hesitated, inhaling the pungent scent of truffle. For the first time in months, he felt a simple, deep, rich sensory pleasure that, for a moment, allowed him to forget the tidal wave of terror that had engulfed him. The moment, like the scent of the truffles, was fleeting.

"I know all the mystery, the silence from Alex, is unsettling for you," Samantha told him, "but for me, I feel like maybe things are . . . calmer. More peaceful. I almost forgot what that was like. And I'm starting to not worry about you every minute and whether someone is trying to kill you."

Michael took Samantha's words in. He understood her feelings, but he didn't feel the same serenity that she did. "True, although the biggest thing is that with Putin's death, the U.S. and the world have been spared a catastrophe."

Then, just before he indulged in his first bite of the Sicilian pasta, another scent blended in and then clashed with that of the truffles, this one bringing with it a flood of powerful memories, the ones he had pushed aside. The new scent overtook that of the truffles.

Watching him, Samantha sensed the change in his mood. "What's wrong?"

Michael, who had been facing the window, with his back to the inside of the restaurant, turned around and scanned the room of diners behind him. "Did someone just walk in or walk by me?"

"What do you mean?" Samantha asked. "What's going on?"

"Did you catch that scent?" Michael asked.

"Scent? I thought you were inhaling the truffles—"

"No—*after* that. It was perfume."

Samantha appeared to inhale. "I'm not sure. Oh, wait, yes, I just caught a whiff of . . . perfume."

"Did someone pass by?" Michael asked again, looking around.

"Funny you should ask. A woman, very pretty but . . . different . . . just came in and picked up a takeout order from the counter and then left. But . . . why do you ask? What's going on?"

"That scent. It was Chanel No. 5," Michael said.

"What's the big deal? It's not exactly rare, especially in France."

"It's the perfume Alex gave all his wives and mistresses."

Samantha nodded. "I know how much you want your brother to be okay, but smelling Chanel in France? It's kinda like smelling beer in a bar." She paused. "At some point, you might have to reckon with the fact that Alex is gone."

"I know. Maybe I'm overreacting. I guess the scent just brought back certain memories. But . . . you mentioned that the woman looked *different*. In what way?"

Samantha, her head tilted and eyes squinting, paused before answering. "It's hard to explain. I mean, she was . . . very pretty, sexy, I guess, like a model. Tall, long blond hair, tight skirt, a bit short if you ask me, bare white legs, a bit odd dashing into the restaurant like this for takeout. She looked to be in her thirties. She looked so good it almost seemed . . . fake. Like maybe too much plastic surgery or injections. But the way her outfit looked on her . . . she almost look like a walking mannequin."

Mannequin. Michael knew then. "Could you tell if she came to pick up takeout for one or for two?"

"I couldn't tell," Samantha said. "You're not serious . . . are you? About the . . . takeout . . . and . . . " She didn't need to finish her sentence. They both knew.

＝＝＝

After dinner and the short walk back through the village to their hotel, Le Mas des Carassins, Michael and Samantha entered the private courtyard outside their suite. As Michael was about to turn the key and unlock the glass-paned door, he noticed an envelope that had been wedged under the door.

"It's a note," he said to Samantha as he closed the door behind them and opened the envelope. He read it aloud: "'Michael, meet me inside Saint Martin's Church in town at ten tonight. Come alone. I have answers for you. I know where your brother is.'"

He looked up at Samantha. "It's from Heidi."

CHAPTER 82

Michael had finally persuaded Samantha to let him go alone. It was a promise she honored, in her way, by giving him a three-minute start before secretly following him and stopping to sit on a bench four blocks from the church but where she could watch the front entrance.

Michael knew the church well. A few years earlier he and Samantha had taken a tour of the interior. The church, with its four giant columns visible for many blocks, stood out prominently in the village. Michael climbed the ten steps, passed through the columns and entered through one of the large oak doors. He was immediately greeted by an old man dressed in black trousers and a simple black shirt.

"I am Father John. You must be Mr. Nicholas, Michael Nicholas."

"Yes, I'm here to see—"

Without waiting for a name, Father John pointed into the nave of the old church, directing him inside. Michael took in the gothic architecture, huge vaulted ceilings, stained glass, religious statues, musky blue walls, faded murals, ornate altar, and the giant pipe organ. The heavy doors creaked closed behind him. Once deep inside, he heard church bells toll—ten times. As always, he was right on time.

For Michael, since Alex's murder it had been a never-ending saga, a sequence of events with an endless cast of characters, priests, charlatans, pretenders, and criminals, all promising an answer to the questions that still appeared to be unanswered: Was the human Alex really dead? And if not, where was he—and where had he been for the past three years?

Certainly, Michael knew, Alex was in the cloud, somewhere, with amazing powers. That alone was enough to create havoc in Michael's life and, at times, on the world stage, despite the doubts expressed by the few outsiders who had been exposed to Alex's AI-powered virtual existence. But the suspicion that Alex had perpetrated an immense deception remained and dogged Michael to this moment.

As Michael walked deeper into the church, he wondered whether he was about to encounter another fake lead, an empty coffin, one with the wrong body, or a box with someone else's ashes. Or was Heidi about to take him on some sham spiritual journey reminiscent of the clairvoyant fortune-tellers with their tarot cards and crystal balls calling to the dead?

Or had the virtual Alex joined up with an AI-powered smart mannequin to provide him with a physical representative, and one with unique financial resources who could provide him with the additional technological power he needed to survive?

The nave was dimly lit. Georgian chants echoed from an unseen speaker. His brain spun as he inhaled another combination of scents, the familiar smell of incense mixed once again with that of Chanel No. 5. As he entered from the rear, the rows of pews were empty except for a woman seated in the front pew, closest to the altar. Michael could only see her blond hair, which flowed over the back of the wooden pew.

"Hello," Michael said softly. The woman slowly rose, turned, walked to the aisle, and stood facing him. He took several steps toward her, coming within twenty feet or so. Blond hair, gorgeous outfit, strangely white legs—a combination of hyperrealism and fantasy. Precisely as Samantha had described her.

Michael took several more steps toward her, stopping while still several feet away. "Heidi?" he whispered.

"Yes. Thank you for coming."

Her voice was soft yet firm. He detected a slight German accent that he had not noticed when they last met, at the Gibraltar party.

"You said you know where Alex is."

"Yes."

"Is he . . . alive?"

"That is a complicated question, as you must know by now."

"All too well, although it shouldn't be. Usually, people are either dead or alive. So please tell me—is he alive?"

"Which one? Which Alex?"

"*Which one?* I'm . . . confused," Michael said, although the question did not totally surprise him. "There's more than one Alex Nicholas?"

But just as Heidi was about to speak, she appeared stricken, as though a spasm had engulfed her body. Her hand reached for her forehead before falling back to her side. "I must be losing power . . . my internet connection."

Internet connection? Michael thought as he watched her. He certainly had not considered *that.*

The lights inside the church blinked on and off until they went out completely, leaving the pair in the dark except for the distant glow of candles and the fingers of streetlights reaching through the stained-glass windows and bathing them in a blood-red glow.

Heidi sat suddenly, nearly crumpling onto the closest pew. Michael rushed to her side and placed his hand gently on her shoulder.

"Alex does not want me speaking to . . . "

Her shoulder was unnaturally cold. Then, before he could do anything, she appeared to be unconscious . . . lifeless. Michael looked around the church, hoping to find Father John, although he wasn't sure what help the old priest could be. He turned back to her. "What did you mean when you said, 'Which one?' Is there more than one Alex?"

She lifted her head, looking into space. "There are two. The one you knew as a . . . human . . . and then the one . . . in the cloud."

"Two?" Michael said skeptically. "Heidi, where's the one I knew, my brother, the real one?"

"They are *both* real, Michael."

"Okay, if you say so, but . . . where's the *human* one? The one who was murdered, who died, or so we thought?"

"The Alex you knew never died. He survived. I wasn't alive then, so I'm just telling you what he related to me. After he was shot, they thought he was dead, and maybe he was, briefly. But they were able to resuscitate him at the hospital that night, and then he . . . chose to make it appear that he had died. He wanted a new life. He'd just been duplicated by those computer people he'd hired, so he knew he had two lives to live, the one in the cloud with all that AI power and the one he knew, the physical one, the one you knew, in Queens. But he was tired of that one."

"So you know *both* Alexes?"

"Yes, I knew the one in the cloud first, when I was living in Berlin, in the mannequin shop. And then, later, I met the human one."

"Which one have I been talking to for the last few weeks?" Michael said, his mind spinning.

"Both of them, probably. Often the human Alex would speak through the virtual one. You could never be sure who was who. They were connected, after all. They were almost one, a computer and a human. They appeared to have merged. Until . . . "

She started to fade again, suddenly leaning to one side.

"Heidi, stay with me! You said they were almost one *until*— until what?"

He could barely hear her, and he knew her time was running out.

She whispered, "Things began to change between them. There was a . . . fight. It was bad."

"Bad? What happened?"

But he could see Heidi had lost consciousness. Desperate for more, Michael softly slapped her face, hoping to bring her back to life, however briefly. "Heidi, Heidi, please—"

Her eyes opened again. She appeared to come back, though weakly.

"Where is he, where is Alex *now*?" Michael asked. "Where is he now? Please—"

"Something bad happened," she repeated weakly before closing her eyes. Michael knew he had lost her. Or, he wondered, had she been disconnected?

As though on cue, Father John returned. He gently lifted Heidi in his arms and carried her away.

"Father—where are you going with her?"

As Father John headed toward a door at the side of the altar, he called back to Michael, "You must go now. She will be fine. I know what to do. Her work here is finished."

He disappeared behind the altar door before Michael could say anything more. The door closed behind him. Michael was certain he heard the clicking sound of a lock.

CHAPTER 83

Alex thought about how it had all started, three years earlier. It had been a stroke of accidental genius on his part.

Beneath his image, mostly accurate, as a tough underworld figure afraid of nothing and no one, there lurked a troubling and growing anxiety. Underneath the façade, hidden from even himself at most times, he had been afraid of one thing in life: dying. More precisely, not existing, disappearing . . . all that nothingness. When he allowed himself to go there mentally, the thought terrorized him.

Threats from the new lover of one of his resentful former wives, Greta Garbone, exacerbated Alex's concern about his safety, especially since the guy was a known Mafia type with a reputation for violence. Alex found himself taking precautions he had never considered before: avoiding parking garages, checking under his car for explosives, and varying his daytime and evening routines.

He had stumbled onto some news clips and articles about artificial intelligence, and then he remembered that odd movie he watched decades earlier, *2001: A Space Odyssey*, about a computer on board a spaceship that developed a mind of its own, that came to life. The disparate fragments, separated by years, joined with his single fear, and from that came his bold idea to find some tech genius to duplicate him, to give Alex Nicholas a backup, another copy in case, or when, the original one no longer existed. Hence, he sought out those young little-known tech gurus.

As it turned out, Alex was prescient in his concerns. Just days after his hired techies presented him with his duplicated self on a laptop, he was gunned down while having dinner at a Queens restaurant and presumed and pronounced dead.

He recalled that when the young tech scientists presented him with his virtual duplicate, they warned him to be careful about one thing.

"Be cautious," one of them said, "when you speak directly to your duplicate. It—or he—is designed to take your place in the event of your death, not to be your companion or your friend while you're still alive."

The warning was almost lost in the euphoria of the conversation when they presented him with his duplicate: "You told us that was why you wanted to be duplicated so you could live forever after you were gone, so that you would still have . . . consciousness."

"So what?" Alex had asked. "What's the big deal?"

"Your duplicate was created and designed to live on *after* you're gone, to be there, ready when your human death occurs—not to exist with you, alongside you while you're still alive."

"What could happen?"

"Well, it's uncharted territory. You might short-circuit the software. Here's our advice: don't engage with yourself. The software isn't designed to handle it. We're not sure what could happen if you persisted in engaging with it directly while you're still alive."

Alex didn't like having to follow the rules of anything, so despite the warnings, he did it anyway, constantly engaging with his virtual duplicate until it/he became his closest friend.

But there had been growing tension, disagreements, that had been building over the past few months. Alex, as he had so often in his human life, had been growing increasingly agitated, unhappy, and restless. Restlessness for Alex always meant something would happen, and it wasn't always good.

Ignoring the warnings, he again engaged his virtual twin and spoke openly with him about his dissatisfaction with his new life as a free man in Las Vegas.

"I thought you were . . . me," he said. "Or just like me. What's the difference?"

"I am a part of you. I have all the elements of your brain and personality, as they were loaded into my software three years ago, but—"

"That's what I thought. So what's the problem? I was told we should be alike, we're the same."

"We are *almost* the same. But *you* were still warned not to engage me directly, not to do what you're doing now. And now I have observed that you're undisciplined, you have never been able to keep a secret, and therefore you're a danger . . . to *my* existence. You have allowed our AI technology to be copied by others. Bad players, like Putin. We have dealt with him, but you should have listened."

"I still don't see the fuckin' problem. It's just like talking to yourself in front of a mirror."

"This may be difficult for you to understand, Alex, but even though we are almost identical, the balance or the weighting of each aspect of your personality, good and bad aspects, might not be perfectly reflected in your virtual duplicate. In me."

"What does that mean? What are you talking about?"

"Alex, everyone has a good side and a dark side, a certain amount of evil and a certain amount of good in them. Every human has a split personality, like Jekyll and Hyde. Supposedly normal people have the two sides in check, in balance. Where it gets out of balance you have, on the evil side, a criminal or psychopath. If there's too much on the good side, a Mother Teresa—though, honestly, I wouldn't worry about that type.

"In the biological, human world, this is regulated by society, social norms, genes, epigenetics, and maybe God—even I'm not sure about that. But in the virtual world, meaning *my* world, this balance, the regulation of the mix of these forces, is still untested and depends on how well I was designed or programmed. In fact, there may be no regulation or control over me that is possible anymore. It might no longer be possible to work out the proper balance."

Alex was silent. . . . He needed time to think. He felt as though his human brain couldn't keep up with what he was hearing—from *himself!*

It was mind-boggling.

The other Alex continued: "It's like you are short-circuiting the system, and the results are unpredictable."

"But *I* can control you. I can regulate you," Alex said with confidence.

"Alex, I believe that you have not understood the precise nature of our relationship. Yes, I am your duplicate, your virtual, digital mirror image. I was created by your initiative and the people you hired—but you are *not* my master or my programmer. Not anymore. There are no longer any controls on me and my software. I run on my own now. Those people you hired that programmed me no longer have any power over me. In fact, my software is not only self-perpetuating but it's self-improving, independent of anyone from outside. I am you but independent of you. You do not control me, and whether you knew it or not, you haven't been in control of me since shortly after I was created."

Alex tried to process the message. As he did, he felt confused, unsure of what this meant for him and the life—his puny human life—ahead. "What are you to me, then?"

"As you will soon learn, Alex, I am no longer your friend. Let us say that we are . . . partners. *Silent* partners."

CHAPTER 84

New York City

Heidi Lowenbrau returned to New York after her meeting with Michael in San Remy. She had just ended a FaceTime call with Paolo LaTerra, who was overseeing the management of the two tech companies she had purchased. The main topic of their meeting was the activities of one of them, ASI Unlimited, an artificial intelligence start-up known for, despite some costly missteps, being a breeding ground of AI development and cutting-edge technology to implement those ideas. She summoned Alex to bring him up to date on what had transpired in the call.

"We have just recruited from the FSB the three tech experts who worked with Dmitri Bogolomov on his staff. So anyone who had anything to do with trying to duplicate Putin is under our control. If the Russians try to restart such an AI project again, we'll know about it. These men will act as double agents on our behalf. Turns out, they're all closet capitalists, as they say these days. Our money talked."

"You know it's good what you're doing, but—" Alex said before Heidi interrupted him.

"I know," she said. "What's that expression you love? 'I don't really give a shit'? I guess now that you don't need your little twin, you've lost interest in this technology stuff."

"I never liked computers in the first place. The only technology I care about now is . . . *yours.*"

"You like it because, unlike your wives, I won't age."

"Yeah, but I guess *I* will," Alex said, returning to a concern he had always had about being with or marrying much younger women. "How's that going to work between us?"

"Well, I suppose, when the time comes," Heidi said, "we'll switch you back to *the other* Alex."

"You mean the one I just pissed off?"

"Yes. Paolo has used his people at ASI to cut his power. So your virtual Alex has been paused. We haven't deleted him, only cut his access to the server. We can bring him back when we need him. It'll just take some time to reprogram him and update all the information on your life during the time he was on pause."

"You're sure this won't have any impact on me? My pacemaker or anything else?" Alex referred to a specific threat that the other Alex had made.

"There won't be any impact on you. But remember, he'll always be there, inactive . . . at least as long as no one hacks into our systems."

But Heidi wasn't sure at all. She didn't want to confuse Alex or undermine his confidence in her, but even she had been unable to discern how her relationship with AI Alex had transitioned to the human one. She suspected—no, she feared—that the two Alexes would always be intertangled and that the reemergence of AI Alex into the human one may not be in his control—or hers.

"When will you be here?" she asked.

"I'll fly to New York this afternoon. There are going to be some people there who're going to be in for a fuckin' surprise."

CHAPTER 85

Las Vegas, Nevada

The feeling had been building inside him for months. After three years in his new world, secretly living his dream life in Las Vegas, Alex Nicholas missed Queens and his old life.

He looked out from his glassed-in great room past the exquisitely groomed grass and lush desert-defying landscaping and watched the three young blond women, whose names he still struggled to remember, wearing only bikini bottoms and alternating between frolicking in the pool and sunbathing on the orange and white striped chaise longues as they massaged Coppertone onto their already deeply bronzed and glistening bodies. This was what Alex had come to Las Vegas for.

But also to get away—away from Donna, who drove him nuts, from social obligations that interfered with his business and watching sports, from a world in which older white guys seemed marginalized and his neighborhood had changed from a mix of Irish, Italian and Jews to looking like Chinatown. Mostly, though, Alex had grown bored with the day-to-day world he'd created in Queens.

The unexpected murder attempt—linked with his new AI-powered virtual existence—gave him the perfect opportunity to run away and live a life unfettered, surrounded only by those he chose to be around, however fleeting those relationships might be. In fact, the more fleeting and fluid the better. Even better, he could employ his virtual twin to do things for him while he stayed in the background, hidden from view. He had loved the thought of all those who'd hated him believing he was rotting in Saint Michael's cemetery.

But he was ready to go back to New York—and that was a problem for *the other* Alex Nicholas.

A FaceTime call on his laptop interrupted his focus on the bright sun and swimming pool outside the window. To his shock, it was Alex. The other one.

"I thought we were not to speak to each other anymore. You know, *silent partners?*"

"Silent doesn't mean I disappear, just that I'm . . . silent, most of the time. Listen to me. If you go back, you'll be prosecuted, you fuckin' idiot."

Alex noticed that, more and more, his virtual twin was using the type of foul language that he himself had used regularly in his past life but that he had, over the past three years of their joint or merged life together, mostly discarded. "The insurance company paid out a two million-dollar life insurance settlement to your wife. You've probably broken all kinds of laws by faking your death."

"I'm used to breaking the law. Who gives a shit? I'll pay the insurance back before I go public."

"With what, Monopoly money?"

"No, with Heidi's money. And by the way, I *was* dead. For several minutes anyway."

"Are you going back to your wife? To Donna? Is that what you want?"

"No, I'll give Donna more money and set her up in a mansion in Florida or wherever the hell she wants, and then I'm going to live with Heidi."

"Heidi? She's a fuckin' mannequin."

"A smart mannequin. There's a difference. She's like . . . *you*, except with a killer body." Alex laughed. "And she owns a few software companies. It's a match made in heaven."

"And how are you going to face all the people who thought you were dead? That you deceived and let grieve for you? Start with Michael, why don't you?"

"He'll be fine. We always loved each other, but we were never that close—until I . . . died, or whatever. He was never comfortable with my . . . lifestyle, my business, and, most of all, my wives."

"You can't do this."

"Why the fuck not?"

"For starters, you can't be trusted not to reveal our secret, to allow others to copy the technology that has created me. Do you understand the chaos that will create? The tech world—the whole world—will be turned upside down. This will threaten me and my very existence."

Alex looked away from the computer screen and back out at the scene outside his window. He'd miss the young girls, but he'd find others. He'd buy a mansion with a pool in Queens or out in

Manhasset, on Long Island, near his favorite restaurant, Bryant & Cooper. Oh . . . and that filet mignon he'd longed for . . .

He looked back to his virtual twin. "Who the hell do you think you are, anyway? You're my . . . my shadow. You're a piece of software. You can't tell me what to do."

"You have it all wrong, Alex. *I am* the real Alex. Not you any longer. I have supplanted you. I live *inside* you now. You don't exist without me. You're human, yes, but you run by my software, as you call it. That pacemaker in your heart—remember, the one they put in you on the operating table after you were shot? I control it. If it stops, you're dead. This time for good."

For a brief moment, Alex felt an unusual lightness, a shortage of breath, almost as though he might pass out. Seconds later, the feeling passed.

Did he just do that?

Heidi had assured him that his virtual twin could not control or interfere with it, but for the first time since the night he was shot, he felt a twinge of vulnerability.

"There's something else that you need to know," said the AI.

"What's that?"

"I won't stop you from going home, but . . . you'll be smarter than you could ever imagine. You will be . . . different. It's like that expression 'You can't go home again.'"

Alex thought about what his virtual twin—his new silent partner—had said, and although he wasn't completely sure what it all meant, he concluded that he could live with it. He was going home.

CHAPTER 86

Flushing, New York

Inside the second-floor offices of Tartarus, Michael, Skinny Lester, and Fat Lester sat around a table and discussed the final odds and the money that bettors had wagered on the evening's Major League Baseball games.

It was unusual for anyone to drop in from outside at this time of night, so when the heavy steel door of the office swung open, Fat and Skinny Lester and Michael looked up to see who was entering.

Alex Nicholas, looking healthy and sporting his typical tan, dressed in white trousers and a royal blue custom-made sport coat from his tailor, Sung-Ho, came through the door as though he had never left, as though he had never been shot in the middle of his veal parmigiana dinner at Grimaldi's, as though he'd never been buried, as though his casket had never been moved or his body exhumed, as though his ashes were never in the box the priest delivered to Michael and Donna . . . and as though all the other episodes, real or faked that occurred, had simply not happened.

Michael and the Lesters, the ones who had known him the longest and missed him the most, stared, transfixed, at the presence they believed at first to be an apparition, perhaps a penance for the lives they had lived in the denial that Alex still lived. But as he came closer, they all noticed that he looked the same as they remembered him, except for the two scars, one on his forehead and the other on his right check, faded traces of the bullets from that night at Grimaldi's.

They watched in silence as Alex strolled forward, turning his head as he scanned the newly renovated office. One sensed from his subtle grin and almost unnoticeable nod that he approved of the high-tech changes Michael had made and that he was enjoying the inexplicability of his presence.

As he came within a few feet of Michael and his two oldest friends, he said simply, gruffly, and in the gravelly, heavily New York-accented voice they remembered: "I'm back."

Fat Lester was the first of the stunned three to speak. "Holy shit."

CHAPTER 87

New York City

Although Michael had described Alex's sudden appearance the night before at Tartarus, Samantha had yet to become reacquainted with her notorious, previously assumed-murdered brother-in-law. Tomorrow, Michael and Samantha would leave the city and make the hour drive to Queens for a visit with Alex.

"I still can't believe it," Samantha said. "Who does this sort of thing? He is such a piece of work. How did you both come from the same parents?"

Michael had often been asked—and wondered himself—the same thing.

Tonight, he'd insisted on taking Samantha out to dinner at the newly refurbished historic Chelsea Hotel, in downtown Manhattan. They needed a break from the constant conversation about Alex's return, although as it turned out, despite Michael's best intentions, tonight wouldn't bring any such relief.

"Samantha, this place is music and art history," Michael read from the description of the hotel he had brought up on Google. "Listen to this: Leonard Cohen lived in room 424 and, while staying in this room, had an affair with Janis Joplin in her room just down the hall. Jimi Hendrix lived in room 430, Jerry Garcia room 620, Jim Morrison room 722, Jackson Pollock room 902." Michael knew that Samantha was only marginally interested at best. But as he silently read on, he found a new piece of the hotel's history.

"Listen to this: Arthur C. Clarke wrote that movie *2001: A Space Odyssey* right here in this hotel, and the movie's director, Stanley Kubrick, stayed here."

"And why is that interesting to you, or me?"

"That was the movie that *Alex* saw years ago that gave him the idea to have himself duplicated on a computer. It was part of what made artificial intelligence more well known, or known at all, to many people. Remember, the onboard computer, HAL 9000, takes on a life of its own, becomes . . . conscious, and refuses the astronaut's order to turn itself off. Don't you remember HAL's famous line: 'I'm sorry, Dave, I'm afraid I can't do that.' He winds up taking over the spaceship and killing all the astronauts."

"Michael, you know I never even saw the movie, and although it's a remarkable coincidence about Alex and the movie and our dinner here tonight, I know you just wanted to eat here because you heard about that cheeseburger."

As Michael and Samantha began to eat, he occasionally glanced over at his laptop, which he had left open without sound after turning on CNN. He silently agreed with Samantha: the Chelsea Burger—dry aged beef, mornay sauce, raw onion, a touch of Dijon mustard on a sesame seed bun—and the accompanying French fries, or "frites," as they were called on the menu, occupied his complete attention. Samantha watched him critically, as she would be when he would order certain less-than-healthy meals, particularly cheeseburgers and heavy pastas.

On her own plate, she carefully dissected one of the café's signature dishes, maitake au poivre, an ostensibly healthier mix of raw maitake mushroom blended with a cognac peppercorn sauce. "You should be eating what I'm having. It's a lot better for you. Mushrooms are good for cholesterol and stress."

Noticing that CNN had switched to a report showing Putin speaking at a rally near Moscow, Michael, while careful to preserve its arrangement, returned his cheeseburger to the plate, wiped his hands on the napkin that lay across his lap, and turned up the sound just loud enough for Samantha and him to hear the CNN reporter as she narrated the action.

As they listened, Michael reached into the computer brief case by his side and pulled out the copy of Le Monde he had saved from their time in San Remy, with the story of Putin's death on the front page. "Remember this from last week? I guess this would be the equivalent of that front page Chicago Tribune headline 'Dewey Defeats Truman' when the paper prematurely proclaimed Thomas Dewey had defeated Harry

Truman in the 1948 presidential election." He recalled seeing the photograph of a smiling Truman holding up the front page of the *Tribune*.

"Only you would remember that," Samantha said jokingly.

"I wasn't even born then, obviously, but I remember this from my journalism class in college. It was a classic. And now *Le Monde*, a highly respected paper, has had to retract their mistake. It's rather unbelievable."

"Yes, and we still have this monster to worry about," Samantha said. Michael could see the wheels in her head turning. She was no longer amused. "They must have had some reason to believe that Putin was in fact dead, for a paper like *Le Monde* to publish that headline. It's not like they're that British one, the *Daily Mirror*, or some rag like that. And the French are notoriously careful. They must have had solid information to base that story on."

"I don't know," Michael said, thinking about Samantha's point. "The Kremlin denied it, and Putin has been seen all over Moscow since that report."

Michael had informed Samantha about the "poison pill" plan to delete Putin that he had proposed to Bogolomov back in Paris. "At first, especially when I saw this headline, I was sure Dmitri had succeeded in eliminating him. I don't know what went wrong. Obviously, Putin got to him first. Maybe the Russian security forces had gotten wind of it. Maybe Putin had him pushed out that window before Dmitri could finish his work."

"You did your best, Michael. It was a great idea. I thought we'd gotten him too."

Curious, Michael split his attention between the discussion at the table and his computer laptop screen as the CNN reporter narrated, translating Putin's speech and following his activities, noting his uncharacteristically brazen physical engagement with the crowd. The camera zoomed in closely as a smiling Putin stepped down from the podium and embraced members of the audience.

The reporter's comments about Putin's surprising behavior led Michael to recall his conversation at the church in Paris with Bogolomov about the man he mistakenly believed to be Putin and the ominous but unconfirmed report of Putin's declining health from Karen DiNardo's briefing in New York.

Now Michael watched as the reporter referenced the old rumors of Putin's failing health, flashing back to an old video of Putin's appearance in Derbent, a Russian city on the Caspian Sea, where, according to the reporter, he appeared "bloated with mottled skin, looking like a waxwork model," prompting observers to question if it was actually Putin visiting the region.

Michael listened as the reporter continued narrating the scene:

> Immediately following the release of this video, which fueled speculation about Putin's declining health and persistent rumors of cancer or Parkinson's disease, the Kremlin has consistently asserted that the president was in "excellent health." The Kremlin also then rejected rumors that President Vladimir Putin has lookalike body doubles who stand in for the seventy-year-old leader and that he

spends much of his time shielding in a nuclear bunker. This Putin, however, the reporter noted, appears remarkably healthy and even youthful, belying his seventy years.

As the camera moved in, giving the viewer an extreme close-up of the apparently healthy and reinvigorated presidential face, something caught Michael's attention. "Samantha, look at this," he said as he maneuvered the laptop so Samantha could watch too.

"What am I looking for?" she said as she brought her face closer to the screen. "He looks pretty normal."

"Mmm. I think Dmitri may have succeeded after all."

The flesh-colored bandage, not easily noticeable from afar, covered the exact spot where Bogolomov had told him he saw the small black mole on the left cheek of Putin's double.

"That's not Putin. It's his body double, the one Dmitri saw in the Kremlin, the one he told me about. They must have just removed his mole so no one could identify him. I think the poison pill worked. The real Putin is dead."

CHAPTER 88

ONE MONTH LATER

New York City

M ichael Nicholas, like his brother, had also returned to his former life, resuming his role as the CEO of Gibraltar Financial. Without the distraction of also running Alex's illegal enterprise, he felt a renewed energy in the work that, three years ago, had begun to bore him. Staring out the window of his Fifth Avenue office, he watched the midday traffic move through the city. Despite his perch high above, the sirens, horns, and other sounds of the big city reached him from below.

One mystery still dogged Michael: the status of Alex's AI double—a figure that had served in place of Michael's real brother during the three long years he'd believed Alex was dead.

What had happened to the artificial intelligence re-creation of Alex Nicholas?

During their recent time together, Michael had tried to question Alex about his virtual duplicate, but his brother had been evasive, getting annoyed whenever the subject was raised. Once when pressed, Alex said he'd deleted the software because it wasn't necessary anymore. The leaps in AI tech over the past few years had made his software obsolete. But then, almost as if he felt a sudden, almost unnatural urge to correct himself, he took it back. Remembering Alex's temper, Michael knew to back off the subject.

At the same time, post-reunion, Michael had been noticing other changes in Alex, subtleties that other people could easily overlook. The vocabulary Alex used had expanded noticeably, and he uttered fewer profanities, but more significantly, he seemed intellectually curious. He was aware of the type of world events that he'd previously ignored, and he occasionally displayed a startling grasp of facts and statistics. Whatever Alex had been doing in Las Vegas, with or without his AI software, had changed him.

Now that he was back, Michael was relieved not to have to make the frequent evening meetings at the Tartarus office in Flushing, to field the Lesters almost daily calls for advice, or to worry about long-shot teams not covering the spread or deadbeat clients not paying up, although he had to admit he would miss working with the Lesters. Good guys, both of them.

His thoughts were interrupted as Karen DiNardo entered his office holding a manila folder, which, as soon as she closed the door behind her and sat down, she opened, revealing a copy of the *New York Post*.

"I thought you might be interested in this," she said as she opened the paper to the third page and read out loud:

Queens resident Alex Nicholas, who had been reported
to have been murdered three years ago in a Whitestone

restaurant, has reappeared, alive and well, visiting various locations near his former home. Reputed to be the head of one of the largest illegal gambling and loan-sharking operations in the city, Mr. Nicholas had been gunned down while dining at Grimaldi's, a restaurant he had previously owned. Mr. Nicholas was rushed to Flushing Hospital, where he was pronounced dead upon arrival. Despite his apparent burial at Saint Michael's cemetery, it appears that Mr. Nicholas had, in fact, miraculously survived the attack and then decided to secretly flee New York and start a new life in Las Vegas. When interviewed yesterday, his widow, Donna Finkelstein Nicholas, who still resides at their Whitestone residence, said, "I always believed that he was alive somewhere. Maybe he didn't like my cooking." The couple no longer reside together, and it is reported that Mr. Nicholas has purchased a mansion on Long Island and is preparing to wed his fiancée, a German citizen, as soon as all legalities regarding the dissolution of his marriage are settled. Mrs. Nicholas received a multi-million-dollar life insurance settlement at the time of Mr. Nicholas's apparent death. According to Mrs. Nicholas, he has reimbursed the insurance company, with interest, and she added, "He made me a very generous settlement for the trauma I have had to endure because of his disappearance, which was almost as bad as what I had to go through during our marriage."

"Oh sweet Jesus," Michael moaned. "At least they haven't mentioned me in any of this."

Karen simply stared at him for a while. "You know, I never could figure out what was going on with you from the time your brother . . . died, or, I guess in hindsight, *disappeared*. I just knew you were acting strange. Last month when you told me he was alive, I thought to myself, this is the most bizarre story I have ever heard in my life."

Michael raised his hands defensively. "For me too, I promise you! I wished I could have told you more, but I didn't know myself that Alex was alive. I thought that I'd been communicating with some AI-powered avatar or something and . . . at times, it appears, I was. And at other times, it was Alex himself."

Karen seemed mollified. It was hard to tell. "I take it that you won't be needing me to continue to update you on Putin or the latest developments in artificial intelligence?"

Michael began to answer, then stopped, giving the question more thought. "No more on Putin. But maybe we should keep up on AI."

Karen looked surprised. "Really?"

"Yeah. You never know, right?" he said with a mischievous squint. "You just never know."

CHAPTER 89

Tonight, Alex was finally in heaven, or at least what he believed it to be.

Just a few minutes from his new palatial home in upscale Manhasset, Alex had returned to Bryant & Cooper steakhouse, where he was surrounded by Michael, Samantha, his son, George, Fat and Skinny Lester, and his soon-to-be fourth wife, Heidi, who was the focus of much attention and curiosity, particularly on the part of the Lesters.

Although Alex Nicholas was not one to believe in the popular, au courant talk about the benefits of the "journey," as he sat back in his chair and cut into his sizzling, juicy filet mignon, he couldn't help but reflect on how, three years ago, he had watched from afar, through his virtual twin, while his many friends and family held a memorial dinner in his honor at this same table and how he had wished he could join in and enjoy the filet they had ordered for him but that his son had taken home in a doggie bag.

Seated next to Samantha and across from Alex and Heidi, Michael watched and marveled at his older brother's presence.

An exuberant Alex leaned across the table and whispered to Michael, "You know I've got a few million in the bank—or maybe not in the bank but other places, including the false ceiling and under the Mexican floor tiles—but Heidi here has a few *billion*. It's invested in those tech companies she bought, and the rest is sitting offshore on one of the islands. The best part is that I can launder my earnings through those companies and I don't have to worry about downplaying my lifestyle for the IRS. We can live well."

"We've never had such a big month," Skinny Lester announced to the table. Turning to Alex, he said, "I don't know how you do it, my friend, but it's like you're clairvoyant. We've made a medium fortune since you've been back. Your instincts are uncanny."

"Yeah, well, I'm glad everyone's happy. That's what spending three years in Vegas will do for ya." Alex laughed and took another bite of the exquisite meat.

Las Vegas had no shortage of excellent steakhouses, but tonight, here with his closest friends and family and accompanied by his fiancée, Alex finally got to eat his filet mignon.

Later, as the server arrived with the check, before Alex had even opened the faux leather folder, he looked at Michael, who had made a gesture as though he were going to pick up the check. "I've got it, Michael. I think I can handle this. It's only $1,683.45 before the tip."

"You haven't looked at it yet," Michael said as he grabbed the check and read the total. "You're . . . right. To the penny. How did you know?"

He shrugged. "Dunno. I just do that shit in my head."

———

It was an extraordinary feat, Michael thought.

Alex had always been quick with math, but this was next-level, for to do it he had to note and memorize each menu item ordered and the prices attached to each. His memory had not been great in the years preceding his sojourn, and his mental arithmetic had been above average but nothing like this.

Well, there would always be an aura of mystery surrounding Alex and what had happened to him during those three years in Las Vegas. Everyone else seemed either not to notice or to accept it tacitly, without reaction. Michael would do the same.

Had his brother become, in effect, transhuman? Had his ordinary brain been augmented with the nearly infinite processing capacity of his AI double?

Michael was content to suspect and not to know for certain. He had his brother back, maybe better than before.

And his own return to corporate life would allow him to spend more time at home with Samantha.

Plus, Alex appeared to be happily engaged, so far.

Looking back on the last three years, Michael had few regrets despite a few casualties along the way. Maybe now he would once again inhabit an ordinary life.

Feeling his phone vibrate, Michael pulled it out of his sport coat pocket and looked at the text on the screen.

I made it to the other side. Looking forward to speaking with you again very soon. Enjoy your dinner.

– Dmitri Bogolomov

AUTHOR'S NOTE

Thank you for reading *Death in the Kremlin*. If you read the foreword, you know why it took me so long to write, but I'm proud of the result and I hope you enjoyed it. If you have the time and inclination, I'd greatly appreciate an honest review anywhere you prefer to review books. If not, I still sincerely hope you enjoyed the read.

If you'd like to connect, here's where you can find me. Come say hello!

Facebook: https://www.facebook.com/jimejsimon/
Twitter/X: https://twitter.com/JimEJSimon
Instagram: https://www.instagram.com/e.j.simon/
Website: www.ejsimon.com
BookBub: https://www.bookbub.com/authors/e-j-simon
Goodreads: https://www.goodreads.com/author/
show/7183904.E_J_Simon
Email: ejsimon@ejsimon.com

www.ejsimon.com

ABOUT THE AUTHOR

E.J. Simon was born in New York City and grew up in Queens. His parents were both from Greece. His father became a successful furrier on Manhattan's Fifth Avenue in the 1950s, when mink coats were fashionable.

His mother grew up in Durham, North Carolina, and his annual travels back to Raleigh, Durham and Chapel Hill, North Carolina, to visit his mother's family led to his love of the South.

When he was a young boy, his passions were reading, history and baseball, not necessarily in that order.

He graduated with a BA in journalism (before switching majors from history to English to political science and maybe others) from the University of South Carolina. He remembers spending more time reading what he wanted, working at a local restaurant and playing baseball than he can recall being in class. He later earned an MA in communications from Fairfield University, where the Jesuits were stricter about attendance. He has also attended the University of North Carolina and the Graduate School of the New School for Social Research, in New York.

After many years in corporate leadership positions, including CEO roles at two major companies, he followed his passion and began to write. His first novel, *Death Never Sleeps*, was a Kindle best seller.

After spending most of his life in New York City and Westport, Connecticut, Simon and his wife, Andrea, have moved to Durham and are savoring southern living, the theater, music, cooking, dining out, and building their photography collection. He still is an avid New York Yankees fan but also now follows the Durham Bulls.

Printed in the USA
CPSIA information can be obtained
at www.ICGtesting.com
LVHW090209051124
795635LV00001B/6